8/14/18

THE SCHEME

To JASMIN

ENJOY MY 1st

NOVEL

James Paul Ell̶

JAMES PAUL 54 e HOTMAIL.com

THE SCHEME

BY

JAMES PAUL ELLISON

www.bookstandpublishing.com

Published by
Bookstand Publishing
Morgan Hill, CA   95037
2041_11

ISBN 978-1-58909-385-0

Printed in the United States of America

ACKNOWLEDGEMENTS

To Isabel, my lovely wife.

CONTENTS

THE SCHEME

It was a hot and muggy night in early July as Jimmy Sinclair drove out of town. He had a weekly dinner date with the 2 people he loved the most.

He entered his parents' rural ranch house on 50 acres about 8 miles east of Tupelo, Mississippi.

Pat and Earl Sinclair were in excellent health. They retired 2 years ago and gave full ownership of their grocery store 'Buffalo Bill's' to their only child.

Jimmy, age 45, carried assorted flowers into his mother's kitchen. Pat knew her son's routine and already had an empty glass vase sitting on the dinner table.

Jimmy spoke as he placed the flowers into the vase and added water from the kitchen sink. "Mom, Kathy and I are getting a divorce."

Pat was hard of hearing. Her current ear piece was on the blink and the new hearing aid had not yet arrived by express mail. She kept peeling the potatoes.

Jimmy stepped closer. "Mom, Kathy and I are getting a divorce! She's just a gold digger."

Pat stopped peeling and looked at her son. "Now that's good news because I never did like her. I suspected she was only after your money!"

Earl walked in carrying the television remote and spoke loudly. "It needs batteries."

Pat turned to her husband of 50 years. "They are in the top left drawer. Our son's getting a divorce. He says she is a gold digger." Pat returned to peeling her 3 potatoes.

Earl searched for the batteries. "I found them. I hope they're not dead. You know, Son, your Mother and I never did like that woman. We strongly suspected that she was a gold digger."

Earl continued to talk loudly as he switched out the batteries. "You and Kathy got hitched mighty too fast. What was it - 2 months? How can you know someone in such a short period of time? I warned you to date longer."

"I wish I had listened to you, Dad. Now it's going to cost me some of my hard earned money to get out of this sham of a marriage."

After dinner the 3 retired to the front porch that over looked the large fish pond that sat below the 2,000 square foot house on the hill.

Jimmy loved coming to his parents place. He knew he had their support no matter what.

"I guess we can't count on having grandchildren anytime soon," said Pat while sipping on a tall glass of iced tea.

Jimmy looked at his loving parents and asked himself, *'Why couldn't I have found true love'?*

"More tea, Son?" asked his father holding the pitcher in his hand. He held out his empty glass and watched half the contents hit the deck as his father shakily filled the glass.

"I'm meeting with Kathy and her lawyer tomorrow morning and we'll try to work out a settlement."

Pat cupped her hand to her ear.

Jimmy spoke again much louder. "I'm meeting with Kathy and her lawyer tomorrow morning and we'll try to work out a settlement."

Jimmy slowly drank his iced tea and thought of John Farran, the hitman, he just hired to kill his gold digging wife.

Later that evening Jimmy drove to his own home on Rutland Road. He parked his old white Honda in the circular driveway next to his greedy wife's new, green, BMW convertible.

He climbed the stairs to the master bedroom. Kathy now slept in the guest room at the end of the hall. Jimmy saw lights coming from under her bedroom door. 'Good night gold digger', he said to himself.

He left the house at 6:45 A.M. and had to be at the grocery store by 7. When Jimmy pulled into the parking lot he spotted Billy Sutton, age 20, exiting his mother's red Chrysler Caravan. He liked his hard working clerk of 9 months.

Jimmy heard from others that Billy was well liked at college. He was a good looking young man. He was tall with close cropped blonde hair and had bright blue eyes.

"Morning, Boss."

"Morning, Billy. While it's on my mind when will you start college again?"

"I took a year off so my pitching arm could heal. I start back in January."

"Any luck in finding that dream car yet?"

"No, Sir. It's hard to save money."

Jimmy chuckled. "Well Billy you could save more if you dated only one girl at a time."

Billy grinned as he picked up some trash in front of the store. "True, Sir, but how do you know which woman is the right one for you?"

"Well you have me there. I sure am no expert," said Jimmy as he unlocked the front door. He turned off the alarm and switched on the lights.

Billy grabbed a white apron and headed in the direction of the storage room.

"Billy, I have to leave at 9:30. I have an important meeting with Kathy and her lawyer at 10."

"Yes, Sir, I know. Mrs. Sinclair called me before I left for work."

"What did she say to you?"

"I like you, Sir, and I don't want to come between you both so I'd rather not tell each of you what the other tells me."

"Okay, Billy, that's understandable but it's my store and I hired you, remember?"

"I know, Sir, but I want to be loyal to both of you."

"Billy, your loyalty is one of your best qualities. I won't put you on the spot."

"Thank you, Sir," said a relieved Billy. "What do you want me to do first?"

Kathy was undecided on what to put on. Should she wear a suit, a dress, or a blouse and skirt? She called her mother for advice.

"Wear the dress," said Carol Cummings, age 56. "Now remember to fight for what is legally yours."

"I will, Mom. I hired a bulldog of an attorney."

She checked her appearance in the full-length mirror located in the hallway. The floral print dress was definitely the right choice.

Kathy brushed her long dark hair and put on red lipstick. She grabbed her purse and headed out the front door. She drove slowly away in her BMW while listening to country music.

John Farran, age 35, with short dark hair and a mustache checked his 'Wheel of Fortune' wrist watch again.

Jimmy Sinclair, his partner in crime was late. The hitman sat in a corner booth, in the dark, away from the other customers in the Hide-Away Bar and waited.

Jimmy sat outside in his old car in front of the dimly lit and smoky bar knowing he was keeping his hitman waiting. He was having mixed feelings. He wanted to kill his wife but then again he didn't.

The hard working grocery store owner just didn't want to give his gold digging, money grubbing wife a huge sum of money for only 11 months of marriage.

Jimmy really hated her for setting him up. He felt she pretended to like him for himself and not for his money. He wanted the same long lasting and loving relationship that his parents have.

Jimmy stepped into the relatively empty bar and walked over to John who was sipping on a Coors Light beer. "Sorry I'm late. I had another argument with Kathy," he lied.

Jimmy ordered a coffee and said, "I know the police will be checking my bank accounts for any transactions once Kathy is killed. I can't have any out of the ordinary withdrawals. So I thought of a good way to give you your required down payment."

"What good way is that?"

"After I visit with Kathy's divorce lawyer I want you to meet me at Summit Bank. I'll give you half of the $30,000 we agreed on and the other half once she is dead."

Sitting across from the unhappily married man was a professional truck driver posing as a hitman.

"Now did you visit my store and check my wife out?"

"Yep. A very attractive woman. She's maybe 15 years younger than you?"

"Kathy's 26 and I'm 45. Can you make it look like a store robbery?" Jimmy asked showing his hitman the headlines of the *Tupelo Business Journal*: 'Rash of Store Robberies – One Owner Shot'.

"That's my work," lied John acting serious as he tried to look convincing as a professional killer. "You want her shot in the head or torso?"

Jimmy looked at his watch, gulped down the last of his coffee and said, "The torso will do. I have to go to our meeting. It starts at 10. I have to pretend I want to settle."

Jimmy and Kathy sat at opposite ends of Attorney Paul Salman's conference table. He read the newspaper about the robberies while she looked out the window.

The city's premiere divorce attorney entered and placed a small file folder on the table. He then sat down next to his new client.

"Morning, Jimmy. I know you want to get this over with so here are our demands."

The meeting was short. It lasted only 10 minutes. Jimmy walked to the elevator, entered one and was gone. She stayed behind talking with her attorney. "I think we will not come to any agreement on who gets what. I think you will have to serve him with the divorce papers, Paul."

"Your husband has no legal grounds to deny you what is legally yours."

"Where's Kathy? Where's Jimmy?" That's all Billy heard from his loyal customers. "They will be back in a few hours," Billy would respond while bagging groceries or ringing their purchases.

He knew that Kathy and Jimmy had loyal and dedicated customers who really cared what was going on in their lives. He ignored the twinge in his arm as he repeatedly performed his duties.

Billy had injured his pitching arm while at a friend's birthday party several months ago. In a strange twist of fate a drunk man fell off a trampoline breaking Billy's right elbow. It resulted in him having surgery. Three large pins were inserted to hold things in place.

Following the orthopedic doctor's instructions to give his arm time to heal he was throwing a baseball lightly every day to his younger brother, Ray.

Billy had some money put away in a savings account at Summit Bank destined for a used car. His ultimate dream car was a new Chevy Camaro with the sport package with the top of the line stereo system.

The store clerk would gently refuse his mother's offers to pick him up in front of his place of employment each day. Instead, Billy liked to walk the 20 or so blocks to Tupelo Chevrolet and search the lot.

If he arrived during business hours the salesmen would not approach. They knew that the star pitcher of the University of Mississippi baseball team was broke.

'*Someday*', Billy would say to himself, '*Someday, I'll drive out of here instead of walking*'.

Billy's younger brother, Ray, who was 14 walked into Buffalo Bill's with their mother. He was happy to see them.

For some reason this day was extra busy and Billy needed help. "Thanks for coming, Brother. Can you please bag the groceries and help carry them out to the cars?"

"Okay," smiled the younger boy excited at the chance to work with his older brother. "Are you staying too, Mom?" asked Billy.

"No. Your father wants me to help him lay new sod in our back yard. Just call when you need a ride."

Both boys gave their mom a big hug and went back to work. "How much will I earn today?" asked Ray.

"I'll talk to Mrs. Sinclair when she gets back from her settlement meeting but I think $8 an hour plus tips."

"Wow! $8 an hour. I can buy something really good with that," said Ray as he carried out 2 bags of groceries for an elderly woman.

Kathy sat in her car and called Buffalo Bill's Grocery Store. Billy Sutton, her trusted clerk of 6 months answered.

"Billy, I'll be there in about 20 minutes to take the deposit to the bank."

"Mrs. Sinclair, your husband just left with this week's deposit. He kept looking at his watch."

'How odd' thought Kathy while waiting at the traffic light in her newly purchased car. *'That's my Friday chore'*.

Jimmy pulled into the far corner of the parking lot at Summit Bank and waited. Suddenly, a white Cadillac pulled up alongside and a gun was thrusted into his face.

The hooded man smiled, "Give me my down payment please!" Jimmy did as instructed and just like that John had his $15,000.

An elderly woman ran over after the Cadillac departed the parking lot. "I saw what happened. I got his license plate number."

John placed his $15,000 under his dresser. He looked at his 'Wheel of Fortune' watch and walked over to the television set in the corner of his one bedroom apartment and turned it on.

He walked over to his microwave oven and made himself some popcorn. 'Show time', John said to no one as he sat down to watch his favorite game show, 'Wheel of Fortune'.

This was a game John was good at. He was quick to solve the puzzles on the display board before most of the show contestants could do so.

He had found his unique watch among many others at a novelty store for $20 while out on one of his truck runs before he got hurt on the job.

At the first commercial John went outside to check his mailbox. Unfortunately there was no mail waiting for him. He was expecting his monthly worker's compensation check as he had been running low on funds – that is until he met his sugar daddy, Jimmy Sinclair.

John returned to his residence failing to notice a young man with a video camera recording his every move. This activity caught the eye of the nosey landlord who spotted the stranger and approached. "I own this property. Can I help you?" quizzed Mr. Martin.

The young man rolled down his window, flashed a gold badge with photo identification and said, "I'm a private investigator. I was hired by an insurance company to document the activities and alleged injuries of your tenant in unit 33. I'm telling you this because my claimant might set you up with a fake slip and fall."

"How long do you plan to be out here?" asked Mr. Martin.

"The insurance company hired me for today only so I'll be gone in a few hours."

The private investigator handed the man his agency card. "In case you ever need a PI."

Mr. Martin took his card and went back inside his office. John's telephone rang. It was the landlord on the other end of the line. "I want to thank you again, John, for helping me around the complex with all the painting and repairs."

"I am glad to do it Mr. Martin. I appreciate the fact that you give me free rent in exchange."

"I called to inform you about a man sitting out front of the building in a gray Volvo filming you checking your mailbox."

"What?"

"Yes. I have his business card. He is from 'I See You Investigations', his name is Roderick Naughton and he mentioned something about an accident."

"Yes. I am out on worker's compensation from a heavy box that fell on me a few months ago. I'll hang up now and pay him a visit."

John placed some newspapers into a trash bag and went outside to the dumpster that was located at the rear of the parking lot. On his return he knocked on the investigator's tinted windows. "I know you are in there, Roderick. Roll down your window now!"

Realizing his cover has been blown Roderick rolled down his window about 4 inches.

"Hand me your video camera before I break this window and yank you out!" demanded an angry John.

The nervous rookie PI did as instructed.

"How long have you been watching me?"

"I started a few hours ago."

"What's on the video camera?"

"Just you riding your bicycle, getting your mail and dumping your trash just now."

"I want you to write in your report that I was home all day and according to the landlord I have back pain."

"This is my first case. I'm just trying to earn enough money to move to Hollywood. I want to be an actor."

"If I were you I would quit now before your next claimant beats you up. Now get out of here!"

The rookie private investigator rolled up his window and quickly departed.

John knocked on Mr. Martin's door. "Thanks for warning me about him."

"Just glad I spotted him when I did."

John walked back to his own unit and threw the small video camera in the trash. He returned to watching reruns of his favorite TV show.

Detective Mike Anderson of the Robbery Division walked into Summit's bank lobby wearing a beige suit and was directed to the robbery victim.

"Are you Jimmy Sinclair?"

"Yes."

"I'm Detective Mike Anderson of Robbery Division. Let's sit down in the manager's office."

The detective wrote everything down on a yellow notepad. "Can you describe what the person looked like?"

"All I saw was a gun in my face."

"What type of gun?"

"A big gun. I was scared!"

"How much money did you have in the two deposit bags?"

"$15,300 in cash and another $2,000 in checks."

"Is that a normal deposit for your grocery store?"

"Yes it is. I make the deposit every Friday morning. We have some long time loyal customers who like to pay in cash. My grandparents opened the store in 1951 and I took over from them just about 2 years ago."

A police officer walks over and hands the detective a slip of paper. Mike reads the note. "Sir, we ran the license plate on the Cadillac. It was stolen a few days ago from the airport."

The bank manager knocks on the door. "Do you know when I can have my office back?"

"Now," Detective Anderson replied. He turned to Jimmy Sinclair and asked, "You provided the arriving officers with all of your information?"

"Yes, Sir, I did."

"Then you're free to go." Mike watched the robbery victim enter his old white Honda and depart the area. The detective turned to the branch manager. "I will need a copy of your exterior video surveillance tapes as soon as possible."

The manager took the lawman's business card and said, "This is our 1st robbery since we opened 8 years ago. I'll work on getting the tapes to you within 24 hours."

Mike said thanks and walked out to his unmarked police cruiser. "Dispatch to Unit 31."

Mike picked up the microphone. "Unit 31 come in."

"Pick up your partner at the Seven-Eleven Store on 5th and Main."

"Unit 31 I copy."

Mike watched a young couple pull up to the bank in a faded green station wagon and enter. They left their German Shepard waiting with the windows rolled halfway down.

Mike thought about his own dog as he backed out of his parking space and drove south to the Seven-Eleven Store.

He picked up his dog at the pound about a year ago. His real name was Lucky but Mike named him Dillinger after the famous gangster from the thirties.

The likeable animal was always quick to greet his master when he arrived at his apartment, which was located above a barn on a farmer's ranch on the outskirts of Tupelo.

It was a great situation – free rent just because the old farmer liked cops. 'Not a bad life', thought Mike as he pulled up to a traffic light.

He realized the young couple in the car in front of him was too busy kissing to notice the traffic light had changed to green.

Mike blew his horn. They looked back and switched lanes to let the officer go by. Mike passed the lovebirds and thought of Amber, his ex-fiancé, living somewhere in New Mexico.

They met while Mike was finishing his 2 year degree in Police Science.

She broke off their relationship because she didn't want to be married to a gun and a badge.

Amber tried desperately to talk Mike out of a career in law enforcement. No dice, Mike ate and slept police work 24/7.

He was half of a team dubbed Laurel and Hardy by his Captain about 8 months ago when the new partner assignments were made.

The 2 men made an odd pair.

Mike, at 32, had short dark hair, blue eyes, stood 6 foot 3 and weighed in at a physically fit 210 pounds.

As he pulled into the parking lot of the Seven-Eleven store out walked his partner, known as Detective Harry Fusco.

Detective Fusco was 53 year old, stood 5 foot 8 and weighed 260 pounds. Not surprisingly, Harry held a large bag of pretzels in front of his huge pot belly as his partner pulled up.

"Hi, Stan," joked Hardy as he climbed in. The 2 detectives then headed toward a witness's house.

Jimmy entered his old Honda and drove straight to the Hide-Away Bar. He

slid into a booth already occupied by
his hitman.

"That was a clever way to give me
my down payment - just fake a robbery."

"I don't want the police to find
any paper trail at my bank," said Jimmy
looking around the bar.

"How do you plan to come up with
my balance once your wife is dead?"

"I'll worry about that when it's
time. What did you do with that stolen
car you took from the airport?"

"I parked the car one floor below
where I took it. How did you know I
stole it from the airport?"

"A witness gave the police the
license plate number. Now that you have
your down payment where and when will
you kill Kathy?"

The waitress walked up and took
Jimmy's drink order. When she left
their table John answered, "It is best
you don't know. I want you to act
naturally if questioned by the police."

Jimmy walked into his crowded
store. He was greeted by a few
customers and his angry wife.

"Why did you take the deposit to
the bank? You know I do that myself.
I've been taking the deposit for over

50 weeks without a problem. You take it just once and we get robbed!"

"I could have been killed."

"Yes, and if you were, I wouldn't have to spend any more of my money on lawyers."

"You mean *my* money!" said Jimmy as he and his wife continued to argue.

Mike and Harry arrived at the witness's house and rang the doorbell. A sign reading 'The Friedman's' hung above the door. Over a cup of coffee and homemade apple pie the 3 discussed the events that occurred earlier in the day.

Mrs. Friedman put her coffee cup down and said, "I was trying to dial a phone number on my cell phone when a white Cadillac zoomed by me and screeched to a halt. I saw a gun being pointed out the window so I wrote the license plate number on my arm.

"Were you alone? Mrs. Friedman?"

"Yes I was."

"What happened next?"

"I saw 2 hands reach out of the Cadillac's window and take 2 deposit bags from the victim who was handing them out his driver's window. The Cadillac then drove off and I ran over to help."

"How did the victim act?" quizzed Harry writing everything down on a white spiral note pad.

"Very, very calm. I was the excited one. More pie, Gentlemen?"

"No thanks. It was very good," said Mike as his partner finished off both of their plates.

"Could you identify the robber's car if you saw it again?" asked Mike as he put his suit jacket on.

"I think so," said Mrs. Friedman, age 75, as she got up from her rocking chair and walked the lawmen to the door.

Once in their unmarked police car Mike asked, "Didn't the witness say the robber reached out with both hands?"

Harry checked his notes. "Yep."

"Then this robbery may have been staged," replied Mike. "The robber put his gun away and reached out with both hands for the deposit bags. Our so-called victim just hands the bags over? He told me he was scared, yet, the witness just said Jimmy was very, very calm."

Kathy pulled her new BMW into a visitor-designated stall. She walked toward the police station wearing tight blue jeans that nicely fit her 5 foot, 5 inch frame.

Kathy kept her weight down to 125 pounds by working out each morning to instructional videos.

The male cops exiting and entering the station just stopped and stared at the natural born beauty.

Kathy walked up to the desk officer on duty. "I have an appointment with Detective Mike Anderson."

A burly man in plain clothes came forward. "I'll escort the lady to Robbery Division."

"Okay, Captain," said the desk officer who directed his attention to the next citizen in line.

"I'm his boss. Captain Dean Masters," announced the lawman as he pushed the elevator button.

"Hi. I'm Kathy Sinclair and I own Buffalo Bill's Grocery Store."

They entered the elevator and the Captain pushed the button for the 3rd floor. As they rode up Kathy could feel his eyes raking her body from head to toe.

The Robbery Division went quiet as their boss and his very attractive guest entered their section.

"Get back to work, haven't you seen a lady before?" barked the captain as he motioned for Kathy to enter interview room number 2.

"I'll track him down for you."

"Thank you, Captain."

Kathy was attracted to Mike as soon as he entered the room.

"Thanks for coming in Mrs. Sinclair. I am Robbery Detective Mike Anderson."

They shook hands and smiled at each other. "I have a partner, Harry Fusco, who at this very moment I can't find so we'll start without him."

"May I have a glass of water, please?"

"Oh, sure, I'll be right back."

Kathy wasn't thirsty at all. She just wanted to check the tight butt on this hunk of a man handling her husband's case.

Mike returned with a small paper cup. "Thank you so much," Kathy smiled as she drank the cool contents.

Mike sat back down. "Oh, I must be thirstier than I thought. May I have another cup, please?" she asked holding the empty cup in her hand.

"Yes, Ma'am. Sorry we only have these small cups."

"It's fine with me if you really don't mind making the trips."

"No, anything to help."

Mike left the room again as Kathy watched him. He returned and this time waited to see if the lady needed more water.

"Please sit," said Kathy. "I'm not thirsty anymore!"

Mike sat back down and began his interview. "I spoke with your husband yesterday about his alleged robbery."

"Alleged - you mean it didn't happen?"

"He was removed of his money but I think he gave it up voluntarily. The witness said the robber had no gun in his hand when your husband just handed over the deposit bags.

"Why would he just hand our money over like that?"

"Mr. Sinclair told me he was scared, yet, the witness made a point of saying just how calm he acted."

Mike shifted gears. "How long have you 2 been married?"

"A year next month. The day we got robbed was our 11th month anniversary. I made those deposits every week for 50 weeks and nothing happened. He does it just once and gets robbed."

"Your husband told me he makes the deposit each week."

"Jimmy is a good liar, Detective."

"How is your marriage?"

"We are getting a divorce. Jimmy offered me $100,000 today. My lawyer says it should be $4 million."

"During the time you 2 have been together has there ever been any violence?"

"Recently Jimmy said he would be better off if I was gone."

"Maybe he has some female on the side," said Mike.

"A few months ago a customer said they saw Jimmy in a restaurant kissing a girl. I confronted him and he didn't deny it. We don't sleep together any more, we don't talk - we just yell at each other."

"Your husband, is he a gambler? Take drugs?"

"No, no, that grocery store is his whole life. He has a few million dollars in his savings account."

"Then why go through all the trouble of staging a robbery if he doesn't need the money?" said Mike.

"I don't know," Kathy replied. "Maybe my husband really was robbed."

Back in her car Kathy called her attorney and obtained a phone number of a private investigator.

Later in the day she drove to a strip mall and sat in a small back office of Economy Travel Agency.

Steve Conners, a handsome man of 45, with a ponytail and beard asked her to sit down.

"Funny place to have a PI office," commented Kathy.

"My sister owns the travel agency and when business is slow I work out front as an agent."

Kathy said, "What I need is for you to find out what my husband is up to. I think you will find him seeing a woman. I brought his photo as instructed and your retainer of a $1,000. Jimmy closes up the store at 9 tonight and 7 tomorrow evening."

"I'll try to go on your husband tonight if I can. What is your cell phone number?"

Kathy wrote it down and Steve walked his attractive client to her car.

"Thanks," said Kathy as she climbed into her vehicle.

Steve handed her his travel agency card. "I don't want him finding a PI card in your purse."

Steve returned to his back office and called the Tupelo Rainbow Convalescent Home. "Hello, this is Steve Connors calling to check on my mother, Valerie Connors, in room 5."

"Oh, hello Steve, this is Angela Robinson. My husband Bob and I bought a trip to Vegas from you."

"Hi, Angela. Did you win?"

"No. We lost about a grand but we sure did have a fun time. The hotel you chose was in a perfect location!"

"Thanks for thinking of Economy Travel. Now about my mother."

"She's doing well. She's playing bingo right now."

"What time will her next meal be served?"

"In about an hour."

"Thanks, Angela. I will be down to say hello to my mother at that time."

Steve called his sister Vicki who lives in Kansas City with an update. "Yes, Sis, I will give mom a big kiss for you when I see her."

"By the way, Brother. Book a flight out there for me. I can stay a week."

"Will work on your request right now."

They made small talk for a few more minutes before saying goodbye. A couple of female travel agents walked over. "Hey, Steve, want to join us for lunch?"

"Not today ladies. I brought my lunch. Thanks for the invite."

After the women left the agency Steve pulled out his favorite meal, a peanut butter and jelly sandwich.

On the computer he typed in 'Kansas City' and started searching for the best airfares.

John was a long-haul truck driver by trade. He hurt his back on his last truck run and was now out on worker's compensation. He made less money but liked the normal life he was leading.

He didn't miss the traffic jams, the truck stop food, the long hours or the heavy lifting. John did miss his trucking friends and his CB radio.

He thought about how lucky he was to have met Jimmy Sinclair.

While playing darts inside The Hide-Away Bar he told Jimmy he was a Green Beret in the Army. He lied about knowing Karate and of killing 5 of the enemy in the Gulf War."

John showed Jimmy his military photo in uniform which was actually his younger brother, Peter - but who could really tell in the dark, smoky atmosphere of the bar.

Jimmy was drunk when he asked John if he wanted to earn $10,000 to kill his gold digging wife.

John jokingly said, "I'll do it for $30,000 cash." That was how much money he needed to buy his own rig and go into business for himself as 'John Farran Trucking'. His motto would be 'Get It There on Time'.

The new rigs were closer to $100,000 but he knew a friend that would sell his truck for $66,000 - $30,000 down and payments of $1,000 a month for 3 years.

John entered the Radio Shack store and selected the top of the line CB radio. He paid cash and flagged down a taxi, since it was too hot to walk back to his apartment.

John was non-violent and had an idea.

He would get $15,000 from Jimmy and the other $15,000 from Kathy by revealing Jimmy's plan to kill her. He would then skip town and start a new life.

Buffalo Bill's Grocery Store closed at 9:00. Jimmy secured all the doors, placed the day's proceeds in the floor safe, activated the alarm, entered his white Honda Accord and departed the area.

Jimmy didn't notice a brown Mazda van following him a few hundred yards back.

He was on the way to meet the love of his life, Donna, age 22. She is the manager of the Moonlight Lingerie Shop and is in love with Jimmy.

She met him last year when he first got married and bought lingerie for his wife. As his marriage slowly fell apart Donna let it be known that she was crazy for him.

Her father left her mom and 3 sisters when she was 8. Donna grew up poor and vowed never to live in a rundown trailer again.

When she turned 18 she left Hattiesburg, Mississippi, for Tupelo and a new life. Donna knew Jimmy was trying to leave his wife. He promised to marry her once his divorce was final.

Jimmy told Donna a few weeks ago that Kathy never loved him and married him for his money and for the large house he lived in.

Jimmy pulled up to Donna's rental house and locked his car. He had a bottle of wine in his hand as he rang her doorbell.

Steve filmed him kissing Donna at the door and later wrote in his report, 'lights out at midnight'.

Steve set his alarm clock for 5:00 A.M. He pulled out his blanket, reclined his front seat and quickly fell asleep.

Jimmy exited the house at 7 and drove back to his store.

Steve followed him to Buffalo Bill's and then traveled to his own office to ran data on the blue Toyota Celica parked in Donna's driveway.

The license plate came back to a Donna Johnson, age 22. Steve made a copy of the video for his client and planned to follow Jimmy when he closed his store that evening.

Jimmy had a surprised visitor. Donna walked into his store at 6:30 P.M. and pretended to shop. She bought a few items and kissed him when the only customer in the store left.

Steve followed the lovebirds to a restaurant, to a movie, and back to Donna's place.

Just like clockwork Jimmy left the love nest at 7:00 A.M. and drove to his store. He later departed after Kathy arrived to take over.

Steve followed his surveillance subject to the Village Inn Restaurant on Green Street. He filmed Jimmy with a man as they ate their breakfast.

Jimmy left first so Steve decided to tail the mystery man. He followed the unknown male riding a bicycle over to his one bedroom apartment in the Fairground Apartment Complex and filmed him enter unit number 33. Steve checked the mailboxes. The name listed for unit 33 was to a John Farran.

Steve checked Donna's house, the store and other known locations but could not locate Jimmy's Honda. He called Kathy and she agreed to come to his travel agency.

Mike received the background check on Jimmy Sinclair. The target was clean - not even a speeding ticket.

He owned a mansion on Rutland Road worth $1 million, a store worth $4 million, and had over $2 million in the bank *so why stage a deposit robbery?*

"Here, Harry, read Jimmy Sinclair's background report. This guy is worth millions."

Harry sat down with a sugar coated donut and started to read the background report. His lieutenant, John Sparks, walked by Mike's desk.

"Boss, why fake a robbery for $15,000 when you are worth millions?" asks Mike.

"Is he married?" questions the lieutenant.

"Yep, but not in a happy relationship."

"Maybe he has a girlfriend and is spending money on her and doesn't want the wife to notice any cash withdrawal activity."

"You have a visitor, Harry," said an officer in uniform. He looked up from reading the background check on Jimmy Sinclair to see a smiling Mrs. Friedman holding a freshly baked apple pie.

"Here you go, Detective – just like you requested," said Mrs. Friedman handing the chubby one her creation.

"Thank you very, very much," Harry replied standing up to take his gift.

"I added extra apples and cinnamon like you wanted."

One of the other detectives in the room shouted, "Get a knife and bring the plates and forks."

Harry wanted the pie all for himself. He told Mrs. Friedman he would come over to her house after work and pick it up.

"I know you told me you would stop by my place after work but I was in the area. I just thought I'd drop it off," beamed the woman with the telltale dustings of flour on the cuffs of her sleeves.

Someone handed Harry a knife and he grudgingly had no choice but to share his dessert with his hungry squad.

Another officer approached the elderly lady. "Can you make me a coconut cream pie with extra bananas on top?"

Harry was not pleased that his new source of desserts was discovered so quickly. Harry saved the last and largest piece of pie for himself.

After everyone had finished and gone back to work Harry escorted the lovely lady out to the lobby.

"Let me see. I have to bake 4 pies and 6 cakes and I get paid $12.00 a dessert. That's $120.00!" exclaimed the delighted Mrs. Friedman holding the empty pie dish in her left hand.

"Mrs. Friedman's Bakery is now open for business," said Harry as he gave the woman a hug and thanked her again for his apple pie. Still hungry, he wandered over to the vending machine and put in 3 quarters. Harry pushed a button and out dropped a Mars bar.

John took a cab to the Tupelo Airport and went inside. He waited a few minutes before walking out to the long term parking lot. He waited and watched all arriving cars and the occupants of each.

John followed one family of 4 into the terminal and made small talk with them. They were headed to Utah for a week of rock climbing.

John walked back out to their Honda van, quickly unlocked the driver's door, popped the ignition and drove off.

Kathy watched Steve's video of Jimmy with Donna and of Jimmy meeting a man named John Farran.

She thought, 'If my husband did stage the robbery he must be spending the stolen money on her but who is this John Farran'?

Steve interrupted her thoughts with the story of how his own wife had cheated on him many years ago and how hard it was to deal with.

Kathy finished watching the video and then said to her private investigator, "I don't really care who he sees. I just want to know what he is up to."

John exited the stolen van and entered Buffalo Bill's Grocery Store. He walked up to Jimmy. "Excuse me, I need bread."

Jimmy looked up from doing paperwork to see, with surprise, his hitman with a smile on his face.

"What are you doing here?" quizzed Jimmy looking around for his clerk.

"I came for more bread," smiled John.

"Bread and rolls are on aisle 4," pointed Jimmy.

"No, more *bread!*" motioned John while rubbing his thumb and forefinger together.

"I gave you $15,000 already."

"I know but all that money is hidden. I need money now for gas, a meal, a movie and popcorn."

Jimmy opened his register and gave him $40. John laughed as he accepted the money.

The hitman left the store and drove directly over to Jimmy's colonial mansion and rang the bell.

Kathy opened her door slightly.

"Yes, can I help you?"

"Kathy, you don't know me but my name is John Farran. I recently had a meeting with your husband at Denny's Restaurant. Jimmy staged a fake robbery over at Summit Bank and gave me $15,000 as a down payment."

"A down payment for what?"

"I don't mean you any harm. I came here in peace. Jimmy hired me to kill you in your store and to make it look like a robbery."

John showed Kathy the newspaper article of the recent rash of store robberies. He showed her a sheet of paper. "Jimmy gave me your shift hours. I don't want to see any harm come your way. I have a plan where no one gets hurt and Jimmy goes to jail."

Kathy now recognized him from the video her PI showed her. She also noticed her husband's handwriting on the slip of paper in the man's hand. "Go on tell me more."

"At the Hide-Away Bar I asked Jimmy, 'Do you want her shot in the head or torso?' and Jimmy said 'The torso'."

"Wow! Jimmy wants be dead?"

"I told him I wanted $30,000. $15,000 now and $15,000 after the hit was done."

"The Summit Bank deposit robbery makes sense now."

"I made him think I was a professional hitman. In reality, I am a truck driver who will haul anything, anywhere, for a price."

"Why would you tell my husband that you're a hitman when you're not?"

"I am trying to buy a rig for the road. It will cost $66,000 and I have no money that's why. At first, I thought why not take Jimmy's $15,000 and just leave town. But then, I saw your mansion, your store and then you. I realized if I left town he would find someone else to do the job or do it himself. With my plan no one gets hurt."

"So what's your plan?" Kathy asked quickly.

"I botch attempts at killing you and leave evidence behind that leads the police to your husband. You help by telling the police that a man has been following you, that you're afraid. If we do this right, Jimmy will be arrested and convicted of attempted murder. You pay me the other $15,000, I buy my rig, I'm back on the road and you are a free and rich woman."

"Why not just go to the police and tell them what's going on?"

"I hate the police."

"You wear a wire, get Jimmy talking, he confirms what you just told me and they arrest him."

"Because I don't get my rig. I get involved with cops who I don't want to get involved with and I'm tied up for months or years in court. So, no, I won't go to the cops."

"Then I will," Kathy said.

"No you won't because I'll deny the whole story, Jimmy will too, and then he'll still hire someone to pump you full of lead in a botched store robbery. The rest of your life, every time a customer enters your store, you will wonder, is he really a customer or a contract killer? My way is safer."

"You are right. What do we do now?" Kathy conceded.

"I'll meet your husband again soon. He will give me instructions and I'll call you after that. Now to make sure you go along with my plan you'll need to give me the other $15,000 now."

"What? Give you more money and then you just leave town. No, I don't think so."

"I won't split on you."

"I don't know that."

"I could be halfway to Texas with the $15,000 I already have. I don't like your husband. I want to see him go to jail."

She finally opens her door all the way.

"Remember, your husband wants you dead. Jimmy said he and his parents have worked too hard to give you half of what he owns. The safe thing to do is to get him arrested for attempted murder and out of your life. I need to know if you are on board with my plan. This is why I am demanding $15,000 cash from you."

"Okay, I agree. I like your scheme. I'll have my mom meet you with cash. She can give you the money out of her savings account. I don't want to leave a money trail like I see criminals do on my favorite crime show, 'The FBI Files'."

They talked for a few minutes more. John said goodbye and walked back to his stolen van and drove away.

Kathy picked up her house phone and called a number. "Economy Travel Agency," said a woman.

"May I speak to Steve, please?"

"I'll take down your number and have him call you."

"Ok, and it's urgent!"

After hanging up, Kathy searched her DVD tape library and popped in a video. The FBI logo came on and a voice said 'True stories of the FBI'.

She was 10 minutes into her show when the phone rang. It was Steve on the other end. "What can I do for you, Kathy?"

"I need your services. I want to hire you to follow my husband 24 hours a day for the next week."

"No problem. It will cost you $5,000 for just me or $8,000 for 2 investigators."

"I need just 1 and you can't tell anyone about this case."

"No problem. When do you want me to start?"

"Tomorrow night. Jimmy closes the grocery store at 9 p.m."

"Okay, no problem. I will need a $1,000 retainer before I start."

"All right. I'll come by your back office before noon tomorrow."

"No problem," Steve said. "I'll be looking forward to seeing you again."

Kathy thought to herself, '*Glad that's out of the way. Now I hope my mother will help me out*'. She called her and agreed to go over for breakfast

at 8 A.M. before going to Buffalo
Bill's at 9.

Mike and Harry reviewed the
exterior video of the robbery outside
of Summit Bank.

From a distance it showed Jimmy's
Honda pulling up. A minute later a
white Cadillac stops suddenly next to
the Honda.

Some large trees blocked the
bank's video cameras from recording the
actual exchange of the deposit bags
between the 2 men.

"Our luck," grumbled Harry
munching on some potato chips as he hit
the stop button on the DVD player.

"Of all the places to park they
have to stop by the trees," groans
Mike.

"Want some chips, Partner?" asked
Harry taking another handful from the
large bag.

Kathy sat at her mom's breakfast
table. "I need you to withdraw $15,000
cash from your bank this morning and
meet a man at a gas station."

"$15,000? Why so much, Honey?"

"Please don't ask any questions,
Mom. When it's all over I'll tell you
everything. His instructions are for
you to go to the Amoco Gas Station on

the corner of Madison and Swift, pull up to the vacuum pumps and lift your hood. He said to be there at 11 A.M."

"$15,000! Are you in danger?" Carol asked with a very worried look on her face.

"Yes, Mom, I am in danger."

"What's wrong? How can I help?"

I need for you to give this man the money and I'll tell you the reason later. It's best you don't know what is going on."

"Okay, Honey. What does this man look like? Does he have a name?"

"His name is Max," lied Kathy. "He's about 35 years old, with short, dark hair and a mustache. When he comes over to you he will ask for a map. Just give him the envelope, close your hood and drive away. Call me at the store after you get home. I love you, Mom. I have to go to the store now."

Kathy gave her mom a kiss on the forehead, picked up her car keys and left the condo.

John drove the stolen van to the meeting location. He arrived early and parked a few hundred yards away in the Wal-Mart parking lot.

John watched Carol pull up in her car, lift the hood and wait. He approached wearing a baseball cap and dark sunglasses.

"Good morning. Do you have a city map?" asked John as he held out his hand.

Carol gave the stranger the large white envelope and said, "Why is my daughter giving you $15,000?"

John took the large envelope and said, "No questions, Lady." John walked away in the direction of the Wal-Mart parking lot.

Kathy met Steve in front of Economy Travel. "Here's your retainer," she said as she handed the PI his money. "Good luck, Steve."

"Okay, no problem, I'll do my best."

Mike picked up his partner at the Seven Eleven Store by the police station. Harry entered the unmarked car with a large open bag of barbecue chips. "Where are we going?"

"To the airport. The police recovered the white Cadillac used in the Summit Bank case. You know, Harry, you've been my partner for 8 months and you're always eating. Don't you ever get full?"

Harry looked over at his muscled, physically fit partner and said, "20 years ago, Mike, I was fit like you."

"Well, Harry, in 20 years I hope I don't look like you!"

They both laughed as they entered the ramp to the interstate.

The stolen Cadillac was parked in the far corner of the airport's long term parking lot.

The ID techs lifted no fingerprints but found assorted papers and food wrappers inside the car.

A uniformed officer approached both detectives. "Tow truck will be here in 20 minutes."

"Who located the Cadillac?" asked Mike as he watched his partner stuff more chips into his mouth.

"The attendant standing over there. Her name's Janet Lee." The officer pointed to a young, attractive, Oriental female.

Mike walked over to the attendant while his partner and the officer shared Harry's bag of chips.

"Hi. I'm Detective Mike Anderson Robbery Division," putting his hand out for Janet to shake.

"Hello. I'm Janet Lee, *Miss* Janet Lee," repeated the pretty young woman stressing the word 'Miss' when she spoke.

"What drew your attention to the stolen car?"

"A motorist complained that the Cadillac was parked too close to her car and she had a hard time getting out. I came over to see for myself and noticed the ignition was broken off."

"What did you do next?"

"I called the police station and the dispatcher told me it was stolen. She asked me to keep an eye on it until a police car could respond."

"Do you have security cameras in this area?" questioned Mike.

"Only on the way out to record our toll ticket transactions."

"Our car thief operates like this: The owner of a car parks in your lot and catches his flight. The thief then steals the car, uses it, and for some strange reason drops the car back off at the airport," said Mike.

"That is strange," said Janet.

"He then steals another car from a new departing passenger catching a flight out of town. When do you show the Cadillac arriving back at the airport?"

"Let me see, here it is, on Thursday afternoon," Janet replied while looking at papers on a clipboard in her hands. "The police department said it was reported stolen on Wednesday night when the owner returned early from a business trip to Chicago."

"Can you get me the videotapes for that time period and drop them off at the police station? Here is my card."

Mike handed Janet his card.

"I will do that right away," Janet said as she took the business card, touching Mike's hand as she did so.

"We can even watch the videos at my place. I live alone."

'Nothing like a subtle woman', smiled Mike to himself. He took out another card, wrote his cell phone number on the back and handed it to Janet.

"It's a date then, Janet. Call me when you have the videos. I'll bring over pizza and we'll review them."

Janet eagerly took his card and put it in her pocket. She then ran back to her office.

Mike watched Janet run and liked what he saw. He turned around and went back to his partner, still talking sports and eating chips.

Back inside her office Janet looked out the window. She watched Mike walk over to his partner and the police officer.

'*One fine man*' thought Janet as she filled in the video tape request form.

She was only 22 when she arrived in Los Angeles from Hong Kong. Her brother invited her to work in his Chinese buffet restaurant. That is where she met, Diane, her roommate.

For several months the girls had a great time browsing the beaches in search of their perfect man.

Diane wanted to expand their quest for their dream man by traveling the United States.

After driving through many states without seeing much more than endless rows of cornfields they made a fateful stop in Tupelo, Mississippi.

Diane met a ruggedly handsome carpenter and decided to change her roommate.

Janet, somewhat disappointed by this sudden turn of events decided to rent a small apartment a few blocks away in anticipation of a break-up.

Running low on money, Janet interviewed with and was hired by the Tupelo Airport. She started working many hours and was getting lonely for a man's company.

Glancing up after completing the video request form she observed Mike. *'Now he's a good candidate'*. Janet watched the detectives enter their police vehicle and depart the area.

At the crime lab a few prints were found on the papers left in the stolen Cadillac.

Mike went through all the evidence and came across a Wal-Mart receipt for an orange windbreaker.

The detective made a copy of the receipt and went searching for his partner. When he couldn't find Harry he drove over to the Wal-Mart store alone.

Mike met with the store manager and showed him the receipt. He was introduced to an elderly clerk who might have sold the orange windbreaker.

After a brief interview with the clerk, Mike went back to the store manager who located the DVD video tapes for the date of purchase.

Mike spent over an hour looking at the tapes. One showed a white Cadillac arriving in the parking lot. The driver appeared to be in his 30's, had a mustache, and short, dark hair.

The next video showed the same white male in the sporting goods section of the store at about the time the orange windbreaker was purchased.

Mike ordered copies of the footage and instructed the manager to drop them off at the police station.

He made a note of the shopper's description and told the store manager that the elderly clerk was of no help. She saw too many customers a day to remember anything of use.

The police dispatcher advised Mike to pick up his partner at 2354 Main Street.

Mike arrived and caught a glimpse of Harry exiting the front door of the Subway Sandwich Shop. The store was located in a strip mall about 2 miles away from the police station.

"How did you get here?" demanded Mike.

"I had a police car drop me off."

"Who did you meet here?"

"Nobody. This store had a 2 for the price of 1 special so I hitched a ride and came here."

"Harry," sighed the exasperated Mike, "I couldn't locate you at the station so I went to Wal-Mart alone."

"Why did you go to Wal-Mart?"

"Because a receipt for the orange windbreaker used in the bank deposit robbery was found in the stolen car."

"Sorry, Partner, I was hungry."

"I looked at the store's videotapes and found a white male driving a white Cadillac at about the time the windbreaker was purchased. I think it may be our suspect."

Mike continued, "He's about 35 years old, 5 foot 10, has short dark hair, a mustache and maybe 180 pounds. The manager will bring the tapes over after they're copied."

Mike pulled into heavy rush hour traffic as his partner started on his second ham and cheese sandwich.

Donna answered her doorbell. There stood Jimmy with flowers and a big smile. She kissed him in the doorway while Steve videoed the whole thing.

She had dinner ready. Donna knew meatloaf was her lover's favorite. "So when will you file the divorce papers?" she asked excitedly.

"I went to see her lawyer last Friday morning. I tried to work out a quick settlement but no dice."

"What does she want?" asked Donna.

Kathy wants 50-50 right down the middle. We've been married 11 months, sleeping in separate beds 5 of those 11 and she wants half of my fortune."

"Sounds high."

"Donna, I cannot give her half of what my grandparents, parents and I have worked so very hard for. No way in hell will I end up giving her that much," emphasized Jimmy.

"What did you see in her anyway?" Donna asked while pouring more red wine into their glasses.

"I was lonely. I had been working day and night for months running that store. She came in and we started dating. I thought she liked me for me."

"People call that love at first sight," said Donna.

"She started as a cashier and later helped me stock shelves. We went to the movies, bowling and on other type dates."

Jimmy continued, "Kathy seemed to like me for me and not for my money. We never went to expensive restaurants. She wouldn't let me buy her jewelry, clothes, nothing. We got married and bam! A 100% turn-around."

"Sounds like she set you up."

"She did. She buys expensive clothes, jewelry, trades her old car in for a BMW convertible, redecorates the mansion and buys her mom a condo using my money. I know she set me up."

"Poor Baby, I would *never* do that to you," lied Donna.

Steve called Kathy and gave his client an update on Jimmy's movements.

"Good, stay with him," Kathy urged. "I need to know how involved he is with her."

"No problem," Steve replied. He waited for the house lights to go out and then set his own alarm clock for 5 in the morning. He reclined his van seat all the way, pulled out his pillow and fell asleep.

The alarm rang loudly and Steve sat up to find Jimmy's white Honda missing. He searched all of Jimmy's usual hangouts but his car could not be located. Steve sighed and thought *'I'll pick him up later'*.

In the meantime, Steve drove over to Wal-Mart to buy some supplies. He exited his car and walked inside the store to find, to his surprise, Jimmy and Donna at the check-out counter.

Steve followed them back to Donna's home and videoed them entering her residence. He opened his thermos and poured himself some coffee.

Kathy pulled up to the restaurant and entered. The hostess said, "Good

54

morning. Welcome to IHOP. How many are there in your party?"

"Two."

"Okay, this way please."

Kathy sat in a corner booth overlooking the parking lot. She witnessed John pulling up in a beige Honda minivan. He slid in across from her and said, "Nice day for a hit!"

Kathy laughed when he said it. "Your van – does it ride nice?"

"It's not my van. I stole it from the airport. I own a bicycle, but yeah, it rides nice."

"Driving a stolen vehicle. Aren't you worried about the cops?"

"Nope. I stole it from a family on a week's vacation so it has not been reported stolen yet."

"Why steal a vehicle? Why not buy your own?"

"I'm saving my money for my own truck rig and if I'm going to attempt to kill you I don't want any vehicles traced back to me. This way I can steal and dump a car anytime I want to."

After ordering their meals, Kathy said, "We have to be careful. Your plan will backfire if the police link us together."

"Being careful is good. Is that the reason why you are wearing the wig and sunglasses today?" asked John.

"Yes. I do not want to be seen with you. This is the last time we meet."

"Do you want your pancakes?" John asked eyeing the 3 buttermilk pancakes sitting on her plate.

"No," responded Kathy. "Eat them if you want" as she continued talking.

In between bites John explained the less Kathy knew the better. This way she looked more convincing when interviewed by the cops.

"After Jimmy is arrested I expect $5,000 more for sticking around instead of leaving town with your money the way you thought I would."

"It will be worth paying you the extra money just to see him behind bars. If our scheme works I'll put the money in a locker at the airport and call you as to where the key will be."

"Our scheme will work. The police can't trace the cell phone I am using," said John.

Kathy wore sunglasses the entire time while inside the restaurant. She removed her red wig after leaving the pancake house parking lot in the car she rented that morning.

Kathy loved watching police shows and how criminals operated. No way was this scheme going to backfire in her face.

For fun, John followed Kathy. He watched her remove the red wig and rearrange her long dark hair at a traffic light.

He laughed as she got back in her own car parked at Rent-a-Wreck and drove off. *'One cautious woman, I like that'*, John thought.

He made an illegal U-turn in the middle of the road and headed back to his apartment.

Sirens blared and multi-colored lights flashed behind him as he drove down Main Street. *'Damn'!* John thought as he pulled over. *'The cop saw me making that illegal U-turn'*.

A heavy-set, older officer exited his patrol car and slowly walked up to the Honda van.

While hiding his face John gunned the engine and took off. He watched the chubby cop dash back to his patrol car.

John quickly turned into a residential neighborhood and made rights and lefts on different streets. He saw an open garage and pulled the van inside and closed it.

John waited a few seconds before slipping out of the side door of the garage. He calmly walked down the street.

"Sir, did you see a beige Honda van speeding past here?" asked the young rookie officer behind the wheel with blue lights flashing.

"Yes, Officer, I did."

"Which way did he go?"

"A white male just turned right at the corner."

"You live here?" asked the officer pointing at the house where the van was hidden.

"Yes, Sir, why?"

"I'll be back to take down your information for my report." The officer then sped off and turned right at the corner.

John calmly walked out of the neighborhood and caught the city bus coming down the street.

The same rookie officer, Danny Hanagan, was red-faced as he spoke to the homeowner who called the police to report a strange beige van parked in her garage.

The officer stood there in the home owner's driveway knowing that the stranger he talked to 20 minutes earlier was his auto thief.

The van wasn't reported stolen yet, but with the ignition popped out and the thief running from the cops there wasn't much room for doubt.

An officer knocked on the front door of Robert Wheeler's residence at 2446 Charing Cross Drive.

A neighbor came out of her house. She told the officer the family was on vacation in Utah and would be back in a few days. The neighbor also confirmed that they drove their beige Honda van to the airport.

This information was relayed to Officer Danny Hanagan who was making out the recovered vehicle report in the Big Oaks neighborhood.

Mike called the airport police and asked how many stolen vehicles were recovered again back at the airport.

A quick check by a clerk found 4 vehicles in 30 days. All had their ignitions popped out, all had Burger King, McDonald and other drive-up food wrappers on the floorboards and all the owners were on extended trips.

Mike asked for the report to be sent to him as soon as possible. He hung up the phone and informed his partner of the news.

The detective then put a call into Janet Lee's office. She was out, but would call him back assured the man on the other end of the phone line.

Mike went down the hall to the 3 vending machines and brought back a Mars Bar. His phone rang as he took a bite.

It was the Auto Theft Bureau informing him of the chase earlier in the day.

"What does that have to do with Robbery Division?" asked Mike to the officer on the other end of the line.

"The owners left their van at the airport in long-term parking. We found their parking ticket above the visor. There are many fast food wrappers strewn about the interior. The suspect is about 35 years old, with dark, short hair and a mustache."

"I'm coming right over," said Mike as he took the last bite of his candy bar. He left the empty wrapper on his partner's desk, who again, not surprisingly, was nowhere to be found.

Jimmy left Donna's house and drove to his store. Kathy was assisting several customers as he walked in.

She nodded as he tensely entered but didn't say a word. All the local customers knew of their upcoming divorce.

Ten months ago they were 2 love birds, holding hands and kissing. Now they were like 2 wild dogs fighting over a bone.

Jimmy went to his back office where he found Billy on the phone. "I hired you to work, not sit on your butt in my chair, in my office, using my phone and on my time," sputtered the agitated store owner.

"Sorry, Sir," Billy gulped. He said a speedy goodbye to someone on the other end, picked up his broom and went out to see Kathy.

Steve parked across the street and waited. He saw his client's BMW and Jimmy's Honda in the parking lot so he knew both were inside.

Janet dialed the Robbery Division and waited for Mike to pick up. She got his voicemail and left him a message.

"Hello, Mike, this is Janet. I got your message to call. My home phone is (662) 555-5555. It's now 2 P.M. I get off at 3 and will be home after that. The videos are ready. I am looking forward to seeing you tonight."

At the Auto Theft Bureau a map of the airport parking lots was taped to the wall. Assorted colored pins were sticking in it.

Detective Joe Honeycut said, "The red pins are the cars stolen over a 4 month period. The blue pins are the same cars that were recovered back at the airport but in a different spot."

Mike walked closer to the map.

"Normally when a car is stolen it's found somewhere else in the State."

"It must be unusual to have stolen cars brought back, right?" asked Mike.

"Sure is. Why park it back at the airport when they can dump the stolen vehicle anywhere they want."

"I have your toll booth videos for the last 4 months. I want to see if we can put a face to the person doing this," Mike offered not wanting to mention Janet's name."

"No Problem."

"When the victim of the Honda van arrives back in town let me interview him. I'll send you a report for your file," instructed Mike.

"That's fine with me. My desk has too many crime files as it is," pointed Joe to his desk scattered with files, papers and other items.

The detectives talked about the high rate of crime to suddenly hit the town.

"It must be all the drugs coming in, said Mike while studying the map on the wall.

ROBBERY

Kathy watched Jimmy leave the store without saying a word. She immediately went to the back door and unlocked it.

Billy was busy stocking shelves and didn't notice Kathy go to the storage room.

She returned to the cashier's area by the front door to help an old lady check out.

John looked at his 'Wheel of Fortune' watch and walked a few blocks to the rear of Buffalo Bill's Grocery Store and entered.

The back door, as planned, was unlocked. He stepped inside the storage area full of boxes and peeked through the little glass pane in the swinging door that led to the interior.

John saw Kathy and an elderly woman but no one else. He knew there was a stock boy but couldn't see him. He waited a few minutes, then opened the plastic bag left for him by Kathy.

He removed Jimmy's firearm, slipped on a black mask, leather gloves, a green baseball cap and a pair of sunglasses. John then nervously walked toward Kathy and the elderly customer.

"Don't anyone move or do anything stupid," commanded John. He was holding a 38 revolver in his right hand. The old woman screamed and ran out the front door.

As planned, Kathy opened the register and started taking out money, dropping some bills to the floor to make it appear as if she was nervous.

Billy peeked around a store aisle and saw John holding a gun. Being a star pitcher on the University of Mississippi baseball team he picked up a large can of baked beans and threw it about 20 feet.

The can struck the robber on the left shoulder. John turned in the clerk's direction and ducked in time to miss a 2nd can of beans from finding its target.

The would-be assassin fired a shot toward the ceiling. The sound of the firearm going off made the clerk duck and run out the front door.

Kathy also ran out the front door as John put 2 rounds high into the wall behind the cash register.

The hitman grabbed all the large bills from the open cash register and dashed out the back door.

John ran into the alley dropping some money and his green ball cap as planned.

He then placed the gun and the other items inside the plastic bag and calmly walked out of the area.

John walked a few blocks and caught a city bus. As he took his seat, police cars with blue lights and sirens drove by. *'Glad the transit system sticks to the posted schedule', he thought to himself.*

The hitman leaned back in his bus seat and reviewed the day's events. The original plan called for him to wait in the unlocked rear stockroom.

Kathy was to tell Billy to get something from the back. John would then tic thc clcrk up, comc to thc front of the store, steal the money, and have Kathy break free as he led her to the storage room.

John was to then shoot 2 rounds off and run out the back door. Kathy was to act terrified when the cops arrived.

He liked the plan but got nervous holding the gun in his hand while standing in the back storage room.

Out of nervousness John just couldn't wait for Billy. *'Almost without a hitch'*, he thought.

The cops set up a perimeter, searched the entire store and canvassed the area looking for witnesses.

A television crew from Channel 6 News arrived and the male reporter started talking to Billy. "So you threw 2 cans at the armed robber?"

"Yes, Sir," stammered the nervous celebrity.

The reporter stepped closer.

"I hit him with a can of Heinz Barbeque Beans in the left shoulder but I was aiming for his head. The 2nd can would have been in the strike zone but the robber ducked."

"Go on," said the rookie reporter.

"He fired a shot at me and I got the heck out of there."

Someone hands to Billy a can of Heinz Baked Beans. He smiles for the camera and holds it up.

Kathy stands outside her store and uses the time to call people. "Mom, the store just got robbed, turn on Channel 6. They're out here covering the crime. Don't worry, I'm all right."

Kathy dials Mike's office.

"Yes, Mrs. Sinclair, I'll get him the message," said the clerk in the Robbery Division.

Jimmy was at Donna's store. He heard the sirens and saw police cars zooming past but didn't pay any attention to this activity. He was too busy watching Donna try on negligees.

"I like the colors but they are not transparent enough," Jimmy said as Donna modeled the new garments that just arrived.

He watched Donna try on more and more sexy outfits as they made small talk. "I really think Kathy's going to file the divorce papers on me this week."

"Why do you think that?"

"Because yesterday afternoon she smiled at me for no reason and said, 'Nice day to be single'."

"Do you want to move in with me and my 2 cats?" asked the ever-eager Donna moving closer to Jimmy as he sat in a chair by the changing room mirror.

"I think I better stay at my house and try to get Kathy to move out. I know we are headed for divorce but I just don't want to file first."

"Why? Donna asked.

"There has never been a divorce in the whole history of my family. It will look better in court if she files."

Donna sat on Jimmy's lap and ran her fingers through his hair as she whispered, "I'll never leave you, Honey."

Down the street Steve continued to work on a crossword puzzle.

Mike arrived and entered the grocery store. Kathy was talking on her cell phone as he approached.

She smiled and in a pleasant voice said, "Hi, Mike."

"I can see from your smile that you're okay."

"Yes. It's been over an hour now giving me time to calm down."

"Do you have a quite location we can do our interview at?"

"The coffee room. I just made a pot. Would you like a cup?" Kathy asked pointing in the direction of the coffee room.

They stood close to each other as Mike asked questions and made notes into his spiral notebook.

"You described the robber as 5 feet 10 inches, medium build, about 180 pounds, with a mustache, wearing a green ball cap, a black ski mask, sunglasses and black gloves. Is that correct?"

"Yes," Kathy replied drinking from a coffee cup.

"You also recall him wearing a green T-shirt with 'On the road again' written in white on the front, blue jeans and cowboy boots, and a 'Wheel of Fortune' watch on his right arm," Mike confirmed.

"Correct," Kathy said.

"You also say the firearm being held in the man's right hand looks exactly like the 38 revolver your husband has at home."

"Yes. It has pearl grips. I did good, right Mike?" she said with a warm smile for the hot looking hunk of a detective standing in front of her.

"Well, I'm not used to this much detail to be honest. I normally get 'All I saw was a big gun'. Not too many people are as observant as you."

Kathy replied, "Well I love cop shows. My favorite is the FBI Files. I tape most of them to watch again when I'm alone which is often."

Mike handed his notebook to a uniformed cop and instructed him to broadcast the description over the air.

The detective turned to another cop and added, "Tell the TV reporter outside to release the information to the public on the green T-shirt with its slogan and the 'Wheel of Fortune' watch."

'These are the best leads going', thought Mike while listening to Kathy talk about an FBI show she watched last night.

An ID technician approached and showed Mike the green baseball cap in a plastic bag.

"What do you have there?"

"This cap was found in the alley next to some dropped money."

Kathy interrupted the tech. "That looks like the cap the robber wore."

She turned to Mike and said, "My husband has a cap just like that!"

Jimmy approached a uniformed officer. "Why all the cop cars?"

"This store was robbed a couple of hours ago."

"Robbed? I'm the owner."

"Then go inside and see Detective Anderson in the blue suit."

Jimmy walked in and noticed his wife talking to Mike in the coffee room. "Everything okay?" he asked with feigned concern.

"Yeah, like you really care." Kathy rolled her eyes and walked away from the 2 men.

"What happened in my store?" questioned Jimmy.

Mike replied, "Sir, you had an armed robbery. The perp fired shots at your wife and stock clerk but no one was hurt. He got away with about $500 and ran out the back door."

"Did you catch the crook?"

"No, not yet."

"This grocery store has been in my family for many years and this was our first serious crime. We've had vandalism, an attempted break-in and shoplifters but never any violence!"

"Tell me something Mr. Sinclair? Your wife said the back door was unlocked. Do you recall unlocking it?"

"Me? No, why would I?"

"Your wife told me the robber must have entered from the back storage room because she was at the register by the front door all day."

"That back door is always locked."

"How would the robber know to come in the back door if it's always locked?" said Mike.

"Beats me," Jimmy responded.

"Your wife said you never warned her about the 3 store robberies that made the paper recently. She said you were reading the newspaper at her attorney's office. Why not?" asked Mike.

"I thought I did. Do you have a description?"

"Sure," said Mike.

"White male, in his thirties, 5' 10, about 180 pounds, with a mustache. He was wearing a green baseball cap, a black ski mask, black gloves, a green T-shirt with 'On the road again' printed on the front, a 'Wheel of Fortune' watch, blue jeans and cowboy boots. He held the firearm in his right hand."

"Wow. That's a pretty detailed description," Jimmy said.

"Your wife provided it."

"Kathy did? She usually has a lousy memory."

"What type of firearm to you own?"

"A Smith and Wesson 38 with pearl grips. Why?"

"Your wife said the robber used the same type of firearm."

"I still can't believe my wife was so descriptive."

"All I can say is that some people under duress, like you for instance, remember 'I only saw a big gun in my face'. One more thing, where were you when the store was robbed 2 hours ago?"

"I was at Wal-Mart on 5th Street in the music department," lied Jimmy.

"Well," said Mike, "We might catch this guy quickly if someone watching the news tonight remembers that green T-shirt or that special watch."

Jimmy walked over to an open display case and selected a cold can of soda. Mike followed.

"One more thing Mr. Sinclair. Your wife says you have a green baseball cap just like the one the robber dropped in the alley."

Mike showed Jimmy the cap sealed in a transparent evidence bag.

"Yes, I have a whole wall collection of hats at home. So?"

"Maybe I can come over and look at the collection. Your cap might have a label attached that we can use to trace where it was purchased."

"Just let me know when and I'll meet you there."

"Later today would be best for me Mr. Sinclair."

"Okay. I'll make myself available."

Jimmy waited for the detective to leave the coffee room. He picked up his cell phone and called a number on a piece of paper stuffed in his wallet.

John was flipping channels in his apartment when the phone rang. "Hello."

"John?"

"Who is this?"

"Jimmy at the store."

"I don't want to talk on the phone. Let's meet." said John in a firm voice.

"You're crazy, hell no. The cops think *I* unlocked the back door!"

"I came in the front," lied John, "and ran out the back."

"Get rid of that green T-shirt and that 'Wheel of Fortune' watch. They are going to be broadcasted tonight on the news," warned Jimmy.

"I can't do that. I bought that watch while on the road and the shirt was a gift from my little brother!"

"At least don't wear them anymore."

"Let's meet," John asked again.

"No, not now, maybe later tonight. I'll call you after I close the store."

Jimmy looked around for Kathy. He saw her outside the store talking to a Channel 6 news reporter.

John hid his green T-shirt under the dresser but kept the 'Wheel of Fortune' watch on his wrist.

The hitman rode the Metro bus to the airport and walked out to the long term parking lot to scan for his next victim.

The toll taker picked up her office phone on the 3rd ring. "Janet speaking."

"Hi, this is Mike."

"Mike who?" Janet asked not recognizing the voice.

"You forgot me already? It's Detective Mike Anderson."

"No, sorry, Mike. I get a lot of calls here in the office. We have 46 staff members and the phone rings off the hook. I just didn't recognize your voice."

They made plans to get together at Janet's place later that night.

John was walking through the airport parking lot when his younger brother called.

"Hey, Brother, it's me."

"Hello, Peter. Sounds like you are calling long distance."

"I am. I'm in Germany."

"On vacation?"

"I'm calling to tell you I accepted my reenlistment bonus."

"Wait a minute, Peter. When you called a few weeks ago you said you were getting out of the military and moving to Phoenix with that girlfriend of yours."

"Sandra ran off with an older guy and the Army offered me a great reenlistment bonus so I took it."

Their phone connection went dead.

John' spotted his next target and approached the couple. He walked over to a well-dressed elderly couple.

They saw the stranger approach.

John saw the old man struggling to remove a large suitcase from the trunk of a new, black Mercedes coupe.

"I'll help you folks," said John. He lifted the heavy suitcase from the trunk and placed it by their feet. "That suitcase is pretty heavy, I'll carry it inside for you."

The couple smiled and said thanks.

"That's a very heavy suitcase. It must weigh over 70 pounds," said John trying to find out where the couple were headed and for how long.

The woman smiled and said. "Our daughter is getting married for the 3rd time in San Francisco. While she's on her 2 week honeymoon we're going to stay at her place and babysit our 2 grandchildren."

They arrived at the Delta check-in counter. "Well, Folks, have a nice flight." John walked away from the couple and returned to the long term parking lot.

He made his way over to the couple's Mercedes. He unlocked it, popped the ignition and drove quickly to the toll booth to pay.

John handed Janet a $5 bill.

"What a beautiful car," gushed Janet while handing him his change.

"Thanks. I just got it," joked John as he took his money and drove away.

"Honey, I forgot my heart pills in the glove box," said the alarmed elderly woman to her husband.

"Don't worry, Dear, I'll get them and be right back," soothed her husband.

The man walked out of the Delta terminal to Row D, Spot 9. The car was gone. The old man rechecked the information he wrote down on a piece of paper in his wallet; Row D, Spot 9.

He searched all the rows with the aid of a maintenance worker riding a golf cart but his Mercedes was gone.

The airport police were quickly called and the tollbooth operators were notified.

Janet picked up her phone, dialed Extension 63 for Security and notified them that a white male just left in a black Mercedes coupe.

She also remembered his comment, 'I just got it'. She told security the guy had a mustache, dark, short hair and wore a white T-shirt.

The police reviewed the video from Janet's security camera and confirmed with the elderly man that it was the same guy who helped him with his luggage just minutes before.

The cops radioed in the stolen car information, while Janet made sure the elderly couple were able to catch the next flight out.

"I don't care about the car. I just want my wife's heart medicine," the distraught elderly man kept telling everyone.

Kathy pulled into the Uptown Cafe parking lot and took a corner booth. She then waited for her PI to arrive.

Steve slid into their booth. "Sorry I'm late but my normal typist is on vacation so I had to type the report myself." He filled Kathy in on what her husband had been up.

She wrote out a check for $2,000 and instructed Steve to stay on Jimmy until she said to stop. She then handed him his check. "When this is all over I'll buy a cruise from you."

Billy was sweeping up the store aisles when his boss told him to take over. He would be back in time to close up.

Jimmy got into the passenger side of Donna's car and they departed the parking lot.

Steve followed them over to Donna's place. He videoed them entering her apartment. The private investigator then started eating another brick, his own slang for a peanut butter and jelly sandwich.

An airliner flew overhead as Steve sat there having his meal and doing his customary crossword puzzle.

He watched the lights of the plane for a while and wondered if Veronica, his ex-wife, was still a flight attendant with Delta.

They were married almost 15 years when she admitted to having a two-year fling with a co-pilot on a 737. She moved out and married the man too.

Steve took a bite of his brick and thought about all of the trips he and his wife made flying stand-by.

His favorite trip was to Vegas. She loved to play slots and see the shows. He liked playing three-card poker. The Mirage hotel on the strip always gave them 50% off their room rates.

After his divorce, Steve sold the house, quit his job as a painter, and moved to Seattle. He stayed with an old high school buddy, Devin Burden, who was a private investigator.

Devin taught Steve all he knew. The private investigator liked working accident reconstruction and taking witness statements.

Steve on the other hand loved working the surveillance side of the business. It was more of a challenge.

His obsession with crossword puzzles came from long hours of sitting in his car waiting for the claimant to do something.

Steve opened his wallet and removed Veronica's photo that he still kept. She was his high school sweetheart.

He was still attracted to what he called the 'Veronica look' which was a tall, slender woman with long dark hair who loved country music.

Steve picked up his cell phone and called his client. Kathy answered her cell on the 3rd ring. "Hey, Kathy, your husband's at Donna's house again. He got here about 10 minutes ago."

"Donna's house? He's supposed to be at the store!" Kathy hung up and called her clerk. "Billy, where's Jimmy?"

"I don't know, Ma'am. He left about 20 minutes ago. He just said he'd be back in time to close."

Kathy hung up with her loyal clerk and called John Farran. "Let us implement the second stage of our scheme. Right this very minute, Jimmy is with his lover, Donna, at her place."

THE DRIVE-BY

John left his apartment, entered his stolen black Mercedes and headed over to Buffalo Bill's Grocery Store.

Kathy went outside to water her plants. It was 8 in the evening and there was a full moon out.

She saw her husband's old Honda coming down the street. Kathy had loaned John her spare key to Jimmy's car.

She turned her back to the road as planned. John rolled down the passenger window and aimed his gun very high as he slowly drove by.

He fired 4 shots from Jimmy's 38 revolver. The same gun Kathy had planted earlier in the store's back room.

She hit the dirt when the shots were fired and rolled around to get real dirty while screaming very loudly.

Several neighbors came running over to make sure Kathy was all right.

Someone called 911 and gave the operator the description of the old Honda. No one got the license plate number. John had blocked out the license tag with an 'I Love Tupelo' sticker which he removed a few blocks away.

The cops arrived almost instantly and secured the crime scene with yellow tape. Kathy gave one of the uniformed officers Mike's business card and asked him to please call the detective.

Kathy pretended to be all shook up as detectives walked around the crime scene interviewing witnesses, taking photos and gathering evidence.

John drove right back to Buffalo Bill's Grocery Store and parked Jimmy's Honda in the same spot as earlier. He then drove off in his stolen car.

The hitman drove the Mercedes back to his apartment and placed a green tarp over it. John placed Kathy's 38 revolver under the dresser and turned on his CB radio.

Donna dropped Jimmy off in front of his store. Billy came running out as soon as he saw his boss. "Sir, the police called. They said for you to get over to your house. Someone just tried to kill your wife!"

"Jesus!" said Jimmy. "Tried! Did they say how?"

"In a drive-by shooting."

You know how to lock up and put the alarm on, right?"

"Yes I do."

"Good, then do it. I'll see you in the morning."

Jimmy ran back to his car and drove away fast. Once out of eyesight of Billy he started driving very slowly.

While following Jimmy at a snail's pace Steve decided to call the store and see if he could find out what was up.

The news of the drive-by shooting was easily extracted from the excited store clerk. Steve called his client.

Kathy answered her cell phone.

"Are you alright? I just heard about the drive-by shooting attempt on your life."

"I'm fine, Steve. A bit shook up but fine."

"Your husband is headed there now, driving slowly I might add."

On the way to his house Jimmy dialed John's cell phone.

"Hello," John said acting tired.

"What happened? What went wrong?" Jimmy questioned.

"I saw Kathy in the yard watering her plants. I stopped, aimed and fired, but when I did, she bent over and I missed."

"Did anyone see you?"

"There were people coming out of their homes when I sped away."

"Where's the car that you used?"

"I dumped it already," said John."

Jimmy pulled to the curb and walked the last 100 yards to his house. It was the closest he could get with police cars parked all over the place.

An ID technician was in the process of removing 4 slugs from the wood siding of the home as Jimmy approached detective Anderson.

"What's going on?" asked Jimmy.

"I was going to ask you the same thing," responded Mike introducing Harry at the same time.

"Your wife says she's scared of you," said Harry while looking directly at Jimmy.

"Scared of me. Why?"

"Too much has been going on since your pending divorce. First, you're robbed in a bank parking lot, second, someone robs the store, third, there's a drive-by shooting, and forth, your comments about you wanting your wife gone!"

"That was just a figure of speech."

"Explain it to me," said Harry.

"I wish she was out of my life but I wouldn't want to see any harm come her way."

"Why not? Then you get to keep the store and the mansion. Weren't you upset last week leaving her lawyer's office?"

"Yes."

"You kept calling Mrs. Sinclair a gold digger because she wanted $4 million instead of the $100,000 you offered her," said Harry.

"I still think $100,000 is fair for being married less than a year. I wouldn't do anything to harm her."

"Do you own any firearms?" interjected Mike.

"Yes. A Smith and Wesson 38 Special."

"Where do you keep it?"

"Under my front seat of my Honda," said Jimmy.

"May I see it please?"

"Yeah, sure."

Both Mike and Jimmy walked to the Honda parked down the street. Jimmy opened his driver's door which wasn't locked.

He reached under his seat. The 38 Special was not there. Mike watched with interest as Jimmy searched the entire car.

"It's missing!" said Jimmy with authentic surprise. "*Where the hell is my gun?*"

"When was the last time you saw it?" asked Mike pulling out his notebook to record Jimmy's response.

"Let's see. I normally keep it at home under my mattress but after I was robbed at the bank I moved it to the car. I last saw it on Saturday morning when I transferred it to my car."

"Do you normally keep your car unlocked with a firearm inside?"

"No. I normally lock it when I get out. I just didn't do it now when I arrived here."

"Okay. Get me the serial number and let us file a stolen firearm's report. Your wife thinks you had something to do with this drive-by shooting. Where were you tonight?"

"I felt like getting out of the store and just drove around."

"Stop anywhere? Can anyone vouch for seeing you?"

"No. I just drove around."

"Do you do that much?"

"No. This was my first time."

Mike writes in big letters: 'FIRST TIME/DRIVES AROUND TOWN/FIREARM MISSING'.

The ID tech walked up. "Looks like 38 slugs, Mike. We'll know for sure at the lab."

Mike looked at Jimmy and said, "38 slugs, the car used in the shooting was an old white Honda, your gun is missing, and you can't account for your whereabouts. Do you know anyone who owns another old Honda like yours?"

"No," Jimmy said, "not off hand."

"A neighbor confirmed an old white Honda just like yours was used in the drive-by shooting tonight."

"Well it wasn't me or my car, that's for sure."

Steve sat down the street watching Jimmy being interviewed by the detectives who wore gold shields around their necks.

Mike walked over to Kathy who was standing with an elderly woman. She introduced Helen Miles to him.

"Did you see anything that went on tonight, Miss Miles?" asked Mike pulling out his notebook.

"Yes. I was sitting on my front porch which is across the street." She pointed as she talked.

"I saw an old white Honda just like the one Jimmy drives slow down and stop. I then heard loud sounds like firecrackers and saw the Honda drive off."

Mike wrote down what she said.

"Did you get a good look at the driver's face?"

"No, it happened too quickly."

"Very good, Miss Miles," said Mike as he wrote the details into his notebook.

Jimmy filled in the stolen gun report including the serial number which he wrote on the owner's manual.

The officer took the report and gave him a case number which Jimmy wrote on a card and placed in his wallet.

The officer walked over to Detective Anderson. "Here is the stolen gun report and I already entered the firearm into NCIC."

Mike took the paper and explained to Kathy who was standing next to him what NCIC stood for.

Kathy smiled and replied, "I know what NCIC is because I watch those FBI shows, remember?"

"Oh, yeah, that's right, you do," laughed Mike.

Jimmy stepped away to be alone. He called his hitman on his cell phone again. John answered on the second ring.

"It's Jimmy. I'm at my house. You failed again to do your job tonight!"

"Hey, shit happens."

"Well the cops are all over me."

"All over you for what?"

They are questioning my whereabouts tonight, the back door of my store being unlocked earlier, that a Honda like mine was used in the drive-by and now about my 38 revolver missing from under my car seat.

"I have your gun." said John.

"You what?"

"I said I have your gun. I took it from your unlocked car."

"Why did you steal my gun?"

"I needed one if I was going to kill your wife in a staged hold-up."

"I need it back right now!"

"Nope. I'm not finished using it yet," John replied raising his voice a little.

"Oh, yes you are. If the cops find it then I'm in very big trouble. The slugs from the store and the wall in front of my house will be matched to my gun!"

"You worry too much Jimmy."

"Why did you use a Honda like mine tonight?"

"It was the only car at the airport I could steal," lied John.

Where are you? We need to meet."

"We won't meet soon and I won't be giving you back your gun until I finish the hit."

"Then you're fired!" Jimmy said raising his voice enough for a few people on the street to look his way.

"You can't fire me. I'm 6 for 6 on hits and if I quit now I won't have a perfect record." John covered his mouth to hide his laugh.

Jimmy paced up and down the sidewalk for a moment before whispering. "Listen. I don't want to kill my wife any more. You can keep the $15,000, just give me back my gun."

"Tell you what. You give me an additional $15,000 tomorrow and I'll give you your gun back."

"And you will leave my wife alone?"

"That I will have to think about. I do have a perfect record."

"I'll get you the money first thing in the morning. Where can we meet?" asked Jimmy.

"There's a dump site off Highway 45, Exit 2. Go east 3 miles, just past the all night Speedway Gas Station and turn left on Victory Lane. I'll be a few yards in at 11 A.M.," replied John.

"I'll be there," said Jimmy as he underlined 11 A.M. on a piece of paper. He had his back to the house and didn't see Harry approaching.

"Who did you fire?" the detective inquired.

"Oh, you heard that did you?"

"Yes. I couldn't help hearing you shout it. I was in my unmarked car just a few feet from you."

"I fired my yard guy, Tony."

"Why may I ask?"

"I'm sick and tired of him doing a sloppy job," lied Jimmy with a straight face.

Kathy sat at her kitchen table and gazed into Mike's blue eyes.

"I just love your blue eyes. You're single, right?"

"Yes I am."

"I'll be single soon too. Jimmy gets served his divorce papers tomorrow."

"Does he know?"

"No. In my heart I know Jimmy's behind this whole thing. He hates me, just *hates* me!"

"I'll call Jimmy in for a real long talk to see where his head is at."

Mike tapped her hand with his, gave Kathy a smile and said softly, "I'll be right back."

He joined his partner on the sidewalk where they talked for a few minutes.

Mike then walked over to Jimmy. "How 'bout we have a talk at the station tomorrow around 11 A.M.?"

"I have a dental appointment at 11." Jimmy quickly lied knowing he had to meet with John at that time to get his gun back.

"Okay, say 3 P.M. then."

"I can make that."

"Good. See you then," said Mike walking back to Kathy.

"Jimmy's coming in to see me at 3 P.M. tomorrow right after his dental appointment at 11."

"A dental appointment? Don't make me laugh. Jimmy hates dentists. He won't go near them."

"Really?"

"It's true," said Kathy.

"Do you know why he fired his gardener, Tony?"

"Gardener, what gardener? We don't have a gardener. I do all the yard work myself to keep in shape."

"Jimmy told my partner he fired his gardener tonight. Harry heard him say to someone over his cell phone, 'You're fired'."

"My soon to be ex is a good liar. Jimmy has a poker face."

Jimmy was walking to his car when Mike yelled for him to come to the house. He walked back wondering what they wanted now.

"Mr. Sinclair can you show me that baseball cap collection of yours?" asked Mike.

Harry stayed outside in the front yard flirting with the ID techs and offering them some of his potato chips.

On one wall of the game room was an assorted collection of baseball caps of different sizes and colors.

"How long have you been collecting these?" asked Mike while looking for a green colored baseball cap.

"I started about 3 years ago. They are orphan hats."

"Orphan hats! What do you mean?" prodded Mike.

"When I am driving around town I look for discarded hats on the side of the road. If I find one I claim it. I call those type of hats, 'orphans'."

"Where's that orphan green baseball cap you said you owned?" asked Mike.

Jimmy walked over to the far section of the wall to a solitary nail where the cap should have been hanging. "That's odd it's missing!" Jimmy looked quizzically as he turned to face Mike.

"Seems like a few things are missing in your life Mr. Sinclair. The gun and now a baseball cap similar to the one dropped at the crime scene."

"Look, Detective, I have nothing to do with anything related to Kathy."

"Relax, Mr. Sinclair. I didn't say you did."

"No, but you're doing a good job of implying that I am involved."

"Well, Mr. Sinclair, as a robbery detective I have to suspect everyone until I can rule them out."

"May I leave now?"

"Of course you may leave."

The store owner quickly entered his car and departed the area with Steve on his tail.

Jimmy called his banker at home and arranged to meet with him first thing in the morning. He was going to make his appointment with John and get his gun back.

Jimmy drove to his store and for the first time realized he might be under surveillance.

Days earlier he spotted a Mazda van near his house, his store and at Donna's place too.

He was aware because he'd been thinking about trading in his old Honda for a new vehicle. Hell, if Kathy could go around town in a BMW he could upgrade as well.

Jimmy pulled into the Shell Gas Station on Green Street and pumped a few cents worth of fuel into his already full tank.

He watched the Mazda van turn into the McDonald's lot next door. He couldn't tell if anyone got out or not.

After pumping some gas Jimmy drove next door to McDonald's to use the drive-up window, but more importantly, to write down the license plate number of the van.

Jimmy went by the vehicle and recorded the plate, 'TRAVEL3'. He drove down the street watching his rear view mirror.

The Mazda van pulled into traffic behind him about 6 cars back in the right lane.

Jimmy drove a few more blocks and stopped at a Starbucks for a coffee latte. The van didn't stop.

He got his drink and drove over to Donna's place. Down the street he noticed the same colored Mazda van already parked.

He knocked on Donna's door. "Let's go for a walk, Honey," said Jimmy as he took a sip of his hot beverage. Donna closed her door and locked it. They held hands as they walked.

"I think I am being followed," Jimmy casually remarked to Donna. "Just act natural. We'll cross the street and walk around the block."

"Followed?"

"There is a beige Mazda van parked at the curb. Look at the tag as we pass it and see if it reads 'TRAVEL3'."

"Who's following you and why?"

"I don't know," Jimmy said nervously as they crossed the street and headed toward their target.

Steve sat in the back seat of the van. His dark window tint concealed him. He laid low as his subject walked slowly by.

Donna looked at the Mazda tag as they strolled down the sidewalk.

"What's the plate number?"

"It's 'TRAVEL3' just like you thought. What are we going to do now?"

"We'll act like we don't know anything. I'll call the police and report a suspicious car and let the cops check him out."

Jimmy picked up his cell phone and made the call. The couple casually strolled around the block and walked back to Donna's place like nothing was wrong.

Steve videoed the lovebirds enter the house. He picked up his notebook and wrote some entries. He then turned on his radio and put the channel on a country station.

He was into his 4th song when 2 flashlights from either side lit him up. A commanding voice said, "Police, step out of your vehicle."

Jimmy and Donna watched from a side bathroom window in the dark as Steve exited his van.

"I'm a PI working on a case. Let me show you my ID."

"Reach for it slowly," stated one of the officers who stood a few feet back ready for anything.

Steve found his state ID card issued by the Division of Licensing and handed it to the young cop in front of him.

"I need to see your driver's license and registration as well."

Steve complied and listened.

"We had a call of a suspicious vehicle parked out here for hours."

"I'm working on a divorce case and my subject is visiting his girlfriend. I can't tell you who or provide you with any more information on the case but I am a licensed private investigator and I have a right to be here."

"Just stand here while my partner verifies your information and if all is in order we will let you go back to work."

"Okay. No problem. By the way, Officer, who called about me?" Steve asked looking now and then at Donna's house.

"Don't know, Sir."

To play it safe he would borrow his sister's gray Toyota Corolla.

"Looks like everything is in order. Here is your driver's license, registration, and PI license back."

Steve took his identification from the older officer. He thanked them both and climbed back inside his van.

Jimmy and Donna watched the man enter his van as the 2 cops departed in their patrol car.

"What do we do now?" Donna asked holding Jimmy's hand.

"We will call a cab and sneak out the back. Let us relax by seeing a movie. I'll tell the driver to pick us up a few blocks from here."

The cab arrived about 20 minutes later and the driver took his passengers to the Medco 10 Cinemas near the mall.

When the show was over they made the cab drive down Donna's street. As they passed the Mazda van they could see a white male with a beard behind the wheel.

"He's still here, now what?" asked Donna.

"I'll get a police friend to run the license plate and see who this guy is."

The cab dropped the couple off where he picked them up at. They climbed over Donna's fence as several neighborhood dogs barked.

"Hey, that was fun sneaking around!" said Donna.

"I am a little worried about that guy out there. Why and how long has he been following me?"

Jimmy left Donna's at about 7 A.M. and drove to his store. The Mazda van followed from a distance.

Kathy drove to her attorney's office and picked up her copy of the divorce papers. She was informed that the process server was on his way over to the store to serve her husband.

Kathy rode the elevator to the lobby. The lift stopped on the 3rd floor and Joseph Cook, of 'Cook's Diner', stepped inside with his 2 youngest grandchildren.

"Hello, Kathy, these are 2 of my 8 grandchildren. Kids, say hello to Mrs. Sinclair."

"Hello," both girls said looking bored.

"My daughter works in the building for Barnhill Mortgage in the commercial loan department. I thought I'd take, Cindy, and Stephanie, for ice cream."

"Yea!" shouted both young girls with renewed energy jumping up and down.

"I haven't seen you or Jimmy in 9 months."

"Jimmy and I are getting a divorce. He gets served with the papers today."

"Sorry to hear that."

Kathy changed the subject. "Joe, you have excellent food. I plan to throw a party at my house soon and I want you to cater it."

"Great. I could use the extra business. How many people are we talking about?"

"I'll call you next week to arrange the details, maybe 50 people, maybe more."

"Wow! Sounds great. Sorry to hear about your divorce."

Kathy sat in her car and read the divorce papers. She wrote in her reminder book, 'Call Joe Cook about the party'. She started to make her guest list and at the top was "Detective Mike Anderson."

Jimmy was busy speaking with customers when a young man walked up. "Are you Mr. Jimmy Sinclair?"

"Yes. I'm Jimmy."

"You have been served." The man handed Jimmy some papers in a white envelope and walked out of the store.

Jimmy put the envelope down and continued to help his customers smiling as he did so.

"You on jury duty?" asked a nice elderly lady buying milk and eggs.

"No, Mrs. Sparks, those are divorce papers. My wife of 11 months wants a divorce."

"Will you be selling the store?"

"No, Mrs. Sparks. I plan to keep it in the family a long, long time and I hope to be of service to you for a long, long time too."

"Mr. Sparks and I have been married 69 years."

"Well, Mrs. Sparks, I wish mine had lasted longer but when 2 people fight all the time it's no fun. In the long run it's best we go our separate ways."

"I plan to be single until I'm at least 40," Billy piped in as he bagged the milk and eggs for Mrs. Sparks.

Jimmy looked at his clerk. "Please take over. I have 2 appointments. I plan to be back by 4." He picked up the white envelope with his name on it and said goodbye.

Jimmy put on dark sunglasses and walked to his Honda in the parking lot. He wore the glasses so he could shift his eyes to look for that Mazda van without turning his head and making it obvious.

Jimmy drove normally but did take several side streets.

He didn't see the Mazda van anymore but did notice a Toyota Corolla following at a distance.

He stopped at Summit Bank and went inside. From a 2nd floor window Jimmy scanned the area and spotted the gray Toyota Corolla parked by a large tree.

He pulled out a small pair of binoculars from his pocket and saw a white male with a beard sitting in the lot across the street.

Jimmy called his friend who answered this time. He waited on the line for the police contact to tell him who the 'Travel3' tag belonged to.

The man came back on the line. "The tag belongs to a travel agency called 'Economy Travel'."

Jimmy wrote down the address and went out the back exit of the bank and flagged down a passing taxi.

He went to Economy Travel. It was full of customers so Jimmy took a seat and waited his turn to be called.

Five minutes later a receptionist directed him to desk 4. Jimmy sat down in front of a nameplate, 'Sally Sig'.

A heavy-set woman with gray hair and thick glasses said, "Hello, I'm Sally, welcome to Economy Travel. How can I help you today?"

Jimmy made small talk and finally asked Sally the question he came in to ask. "I was here last week and spoke to a man with a beard. He drives a Mazda Van. Does he still work here?"

"Man with a beard, let me think. The only man with a beard is an outside agent named Steve. He's the owner's brother. His name is Steve Conners."

"Can I speak with him?"

"He's a full-time private investigator and has an office in the back. He works out front with me only a few hours a week selling cruises."

"He must be very busy if he is a private investigator."

"I think so. I haven't seen him for days now. He said he was working a case around the clock."

Sally asked Jimmy to fill out a customer card and that she would get back to him about his Vegas trip.

He filled in the card with the wrong information and left. Jimmy climbed back into the waiting taxi and returned to the rear entrance of Summit Bank. He exited the front of the building and returned to his car and left.

The gray Toyota followed from a distance. Jimmy's mind was racing as he drove, '*OK, Mr. PI, who hired you and why*'?"

Jimmy pulled up to Wal-Mart and went inside. He saw the PI sitting in his car eyeing Jimmy's Honda. He went out the garden side exit and walked to the next plaza where Donna was waiting.

"Am I late?"

"No, Honey. You came quicker than I thought when I called. I have a PI on my tail and I want to lose him. I'll drop you off at your shop and come back in a few hours to pick you up. You can then drive me back to Wal-Mart."

"A PI? Is that who has been following you? Why would a PI be following you for?"

"I don't know yet but I have an idea my wife hired him. But then again, why would she?"

"Good question. Why would she?" repeated Donna.

"Kathy doesn't care what I do - she knows about you. I told her weeks ago, said Jimmy giving Donna a kiss."

He dropped Donna off and drove to his 11 A.M. appointment. He followed the directions John gave him earlier and pulled up behind his hitman, who was sitting in his stolen black Mercedes.

"Did you bring my money?"

"Not yet. I haven't had time. I have a PI following me around town. I had to lose him first to meet you."

"A PI's following you - really?"

"Yep. I spotted his van yesterday. A police department friend ran the tag and it came back to Economy Travel. I went there and a travel agent, Sally Sig, told me who he is."

"What did this woman say?"

"His name is Steve Conners and his office is in the back of his sister's store. He's sitting at Wal-Mart right now watching my car."

"Whose car is this?"

"Donna's, a friend of mine. I also got served with divorce papers this morning."

"Lucky you! When can you get me my money?"

"I don't know when. I also don't want you to kill my wife. There is too much police heat. I want my gun back also."

"You sure do have a lot of wants Jimmy. Well I have wants of my own. I want my $15,000 and I want it now, PI

110

on your ass or not. I'm giving you until tomorrow night."

"I'll give you the money but I need my gun back and your word you will leave Kathy alone."

"You bring me my money, all of it, and I'll give you your gun back."

"And you will leave Kathy alone?"

"Yes. I'll leave her alone. You have my word."

Jimmy stuck his hand out and they shook hands. He got in Donna's car and headed back to her store.

John dialed Kathy on his cell phone. "Last night Jimmy fired me and just now we met. I had to give him my word to leave you alone. We even shook hands on it, like it was a contract or something."

"Give me the details please."

"Jimmy wanted his gun back. The one you gave me but he thinks I took from his car. He says the police believe he has something to do with the drive-by shooting and story robbery. He wants to call off his hit on you."

Kathy laughed. "Well, a detective heard him last night tell someone they were fired over his cell phone. They asked who, and Jimmy said Tony, his gardener. We don't have a gardener. I do all the yard work," said Kathy.

"You told the detectives you have no yard man?"

"Yes I told them. They know now that Jimmy's a liar. This helps us out because when they bring him in for questioning he will lie some more.

"True."

"Where is Jimmy now?"

"He knows a PI is following him. Jimmy switched cars to meet me. He said the man's name is Steve Conners and he is at Wal-Mart watching his car."

'So Jimmy knows about Steve. I'll warn him to be careful', thought Kathy to herself.

"Oh, I served Jimmy with divorce papers today," said Kathy.

"I know. He told me during our conversation. I replied, 'lucky you'. Now Kathy, go find a house you can rent."

"A house to rent. Why?"

"Because I want you to go into hiding. I want the police to think you're afraid of your husband."

"Great idea. Oh, I am so scared of him!" laughed Kathy. After hanging up with John she called Steve. "Jimmy knows about you."

"He does not. He's in Wal-Mart, shopping."

"No. He has Donna's car and is headed back to Wal-Mart now to pick up his Honda."

"What? How do you know he's in Donna's car?" asked the puzzled investigator.

"I spotted him dropping her off at her shop," lied Kathy.

"I'll switch out cars again."

"I just don't want him to know I hired you."

"No problem. I'll make it look like Donna hired me to see if he is cheating."

"Good idea, Steve."

"Now Kathy, you should tell him you think a PI in a Mazda van is following you. That will really confuse your husband."

"I will do that. I'm going to Buffalo Bill's now. I'll tell Jimmy about a beige Mazda following me around town today. It should be fun to see his expression when I do!"

Jimmy and Donna drove around the Wal-Mart parking lot but spotted no surveillance vehicles or a bearded man sitting in any car.

Jimmy went into Wal-Mart via the garden center and walked out the front doors to his car. He drove back to the grocery store and saw no vehicles following him.

He walked into his store as Billy approached. "Mr. Sinclair, your wife is a nervous wreck. A man has been following her around in a beige Mazda van. Mrs. Sinclair says he has a beard, baseball cap and sunglasses. I went outside but he was already gone. Your wife thinks you hired him!"

Jimmy pulled Kathy aside and she told him about the Mazda van. He then told her the same man had been following him yesterday and today as well. He knew the man's name and where his office was."

"Really!"

"Yes. There's a fat lady, Sally Sig, at Economy Travel Agency who told me the Mazda van owner is a private investigator. I'll go see her right now. I know she'll tell me what I want to know."

Jimmy left the store and Kathy called Steve. "A travel agent, Sally Sig, told Jimmy you are a PI."

"Thanks. I'll call her and have her mention Donna's name as my client."

Steve hung up and called his co-worker. "Hi, Sally, this is Steve. Listen, the man I'm watching knows he's being followed and is on his way to see you."

"To see me? Why?"

"Because you told him I was a PI and not a travel agent. I need you to help me."

"How can I help, Steve?"

"Pretend you don't know what's going on. If he asks you about why I'm following him, say I told you about my client, Donna, who suspects her boyfriend of cheating," said Steve.

"I'll do whatever you tell me to do."

"Good. Now he's on his way. When he leaves your desk call me back."

"I will."

"Be sure to act surprised when he comes in," Steve instructed.

"I will. I am sorry I told him you are a PI."

"Remember, from now on I am a travel agent and not a private investigator."

Jimmy walked into the travel agency and went straight to Sally's desk which had an empty seat. He sat down and said, "Hi. Remember me and my trip to Vegas?"

"Yes I remember you."

"Any luck on my trip to Vegas?"

"I have been so busy I haven't had a chance to research your trip." Sally found his inquiry card, "Larry Carmody, correct?"

"Correct. Is Steve in yet?"

"Not yet, but I can call him on his cell."

"No, it's all right. I'll come back another time. He must be busy on his round-the-clock case you mentioned."

"He sure is. Steve's trying to collect payment from his client. He said she hired him to follow her boyfriend to see if he had another girlfriend. He owns a big store."

"Really! A grocery store?"

"I'm not sure the type of store. I just know his client's name is Donna."

Jimmy about fell out of his chair. *'Donna is having me followed'!* He just couldn't believe it. He looked at his watch, "Well, I'll come back tomorrow." He said goodbye and left.

'What was going on? Did Donna hire this guy? Why would the PI follow Kathy also'? Jimmy thought about all of this as he drove back to his store.

Sally called Steve back. "I did just like you instructed. You could tell he was puzzled."

"Thanks. Remember I'm an agent."

"I'll keep my mouth shut I promise."

Steve hung up with Sally and called his client back. "He's on his way and I strongly believe he feels Donna hired me to follow him."

"Good. The more confused he is the better."

Jimmy entered his store and went up to his wife who was standing in an aisle doing inventory.

"I got your present this morning!" he said waving the white envelope around.

"We don't get along. You don't love me and I don't love you. We'll just go our separate ways and split everything 50-50 just like my lawyer said."

"Your lawyer can kiss my ass. I'll offer you a million dollars right now. You take my money, your BMW and head out of town and I'll write the check today."

"Why a million? I am a gold digger remember! If I play my cards right, my lawyer said I should receive 4 million dollars or more?"

"You greedy bitch. I'll tell you what – you might not live to see a dime!"

Kathy laughed and turned to Jimmy with a very cool smile on her face.

"I know you hired someone to kill me. He drives a beige Mazda van. I told Detective Anderson that your deposit robbery and the store robbery were no accidents and that you were behind this. Now I am going to call the detective and say you just threatened me."

Kathy started to walk by Jimmy when he grabbed her left arm.

"You're hurting me," said Kathy." She picked up a can of tomatoes and started hitting her own left arm as hard as she could over and over again. She started shouting, "Let go of me, you're hurting me!"

Kathy put the can back on a shelf just as Billy and a male customer turned the corner.

"Boss. Let go of her right now!" said an obviously upset Billy edging closer.

Kathy was crying now, her fake tears rolling down her face. "Jimmy punched my arm many times", lied Kathy pointing to her red left arm.

Jimmy raised both of his hands up and backed away. "I didn't touch her." He quickly left the store, got in his Honda and departed the area.

Jimmy failed to see a white Mercury following him from a safe distance. Steve now had a helper, Aaron, driving a cream-colored Ford pickup truck.

Kathy called the police department. An officer took the assault report over the phone and promised to send a copy of the incident over to Detective Anderson. She added Billy and the customer, Howard Hines, to the report as witnesses.

Kathy hung up the receiver and turned to both men. "Thank you."

Both men said, "You welcome."

"I need some ice please."

"I'll get it for you," Billy said as he ran down the aisle.

"How are your wife and kids Howard?" asked Kathy while she rubbed her sore arm.

"We are getting a divorce as well. I live with my parents now. Imagine, me at 55 living with my parents."

"I'll probably move in with my mom soon too."

Billy returned with some ice wrapped in a towel and handed it over to his boss. "Do I have job security?"

"Yes. About 4 months ago when we were still getting along Jimmy told me, 'Billy's the best employee I ever had. He's reliable and never needs supervision'."

"Thanks, Mrs. Sinclair. I really need the money for school and a car."

THE INTERVIEW

Jimmy drove over to the police station for his 3 P.M. scheduled appointment. He sat in his car and practiced smiling in his rear view mirror.

He entered the police station where he was directed by the desk officer to go to the 5th floor. The elevator doors opened and there stood the 2 detectives. Mike had a file in his hand and Harry was eating a donut.

Mike motioned with his hands as he spoke, "Afternoon, Mr. Sinclair. We are going to be in room 2. Care for something to drink or eat?"

"I would like a sprinkled donut, said Jimmy as he watched Harry eating one."

They sat around the conference table making small talk. Mike then said, "Mr. Sinclair I want to thank you for coming down to the station today. You are free to leave at any time. I hope you can assist us in the rash of crimes that have occurred in your family lately."

"Can we talk alone? I don't like your partner sitting there staring. It makes me uncomfortable."

"Sure. You don't mind leaving for awhile do you?"

"No, not at all," said Harry.

As he left the room Mike looked at Jimmy. "My partner doesn't like you because he thinks you hired a hitman. Me, I am keeping an open mind."

Jimmy attempted to absolve himself. "I recently was served with divorce papers and it's true our relationship is over. Kathy might get a lot of money in the divorce but I don't want to see any harm come to her."

"Then who would want to kill her?"

"I don't know. We haven't really been a couple for months and I have no clue about her social life."

"Mrs. Sinclair says you have a girlfriend?"

"More like a good friend."

"Are you having sexual relations with this good friend of yours?"

"I don't have to answer that."

"No you don't but sex is a strong motive in having your wife killed. You can spend more time with your friend and not pay your wife any money in a divorce."

"I offered Kathy $1 million today. Does that sound like I want her harmed?"

"How generous of you."

Mike continued his questioning.

"Let's go back a week or so. You have an argument at her attorney's office, you get robbed of $15,000, your store gets robbed, the store's back door is left unlocked, your gun is missing – coincidentally the same type caliber used in both the store robbery and then the drive-by shooting, you can't account for your whereabouts and earlier today in your store you assaulted your wife. Have I left anything out?"

"I didn't assault her. I just grabbed her arm and Kathy hit herself with a can of tomatoes."

"The witnesses say they saw you with a tight grip on your wife's arm. Kathy was crying and her arm was red and swollen. They said nothing about a can of tomatoes," said Mike looking at his notes. "Your wife told me she is afraid of you."

"Afraid of me. She should be afraid of John!" Jimmy realized too late what he just said.

"Who's John?" Mike asked getting in Jimmy's face.

Jimmy didn't answer the question.

"You haven't done something stupid like hire a hitman to kill your wife have you?"

"What? That's crazy. I told you. I offered Kathy $1 million."

"Isn't it true you care more about the store than your wife's safety?"

"Yes it's true. The store has been in my family many, many years and I want to keep it that way at any cost." Again Jimmy realized what he just said and again it was too late.

"At any cost Mr. Sinclair, at *any cost?* Sounds like you are desperate. You told my partner you fired your gardener but according to your wife you don't have a gardener. Did you lie to my partner?"

"Yes I lied about that but I'm not lying now about wanting to harm Kathy."

"You told me you had an 11 A.M. dental appointment but you don't like dentists so that was a lie too."

"Yes that was a lie too but I am telling you the truth now about not wanting to kill Kathy."

"You didn't have a dental appointment so where were you?"

"Let me think. I was at the Wal-Mart store in their garden section."

"If I have security at the store pull the surveillance tapes I will see you in the store?"

"Yes. I was in the garden section and then I went next door."

"Were you with anyone?"

"No. I was alone."

"If we look at the earlier surveillance tapes on the day of the store robbery I will see you in Wal-Mart buying country CD's like you told me you were?"

"No. I lied. I was really at my friend's Moonlight Lingerie Shop."

"You lied again but you want me to believe you now about not wanting to kill your wife?"

"I lied because I do not want to involve Donna in my personal problems."

"Like it or not she's involved and I'll be seeing her shortly. Tell her to expect my visit when you call Donna to say you miss and love her."

"I do love her and I will marry her once my divorce is final."

"That's motive enough to have Kathy killed. Does Donna own an old, white Honda?"

"Donna drives a blue in color Toyota Celica and she wouldn't harm Kathy."

"Why not? With Mrs. Sinclair out of the way she can marry you quicker. You also save at least $1 million dollars if there is no divorce. That's a solid motive in my book!"

Harry entered the room and handed his partner a document.

Mike shows Jimmy the document. "The crime lab report confirms the bullets found at your store robbery and the drive-by shooting are from the same gun. Someone wants your wife dead and originally wanted it to look like a store robbery."

"I'm leaving now." Jimmy got up to leave but was blocked by Mike.

"You should obtain a lawyer Mr. Sinclair. The crime lab results make me join my partner in thinking you are behind this crime spree."

"I know I haven't been completely honest about everything but this time I'm telling you the truth. I have not hired anyone to kill my wife."

Jimmy exited the interview room and quickly left the police station. He was unaware that Harry was watching from a 3rd floor window while eating a sugar donut.

Mike located his hungry partner and spoke as Jimmy drove off in his Honda. "He's dirty."

The store owner drove down Main Street not knowing Steve and his helper, Aaron, were following him.

Jimmy called John from his cell phone.

"Hello."

"John, this is Jimmy. I just left the police station."

"How did it go?"

"They think I had something to do with my store robbery and drive-by shooting."

"You did. You hired me."

"Well it's over - you hear me? It's over! I'm going to the bank right now to get you the money. You return my gun and leave Kathy alone."

"The gun will cost you $15,000 and leaving your wife alone and ruining my perfect 6 for 6 killing record will cost you an additional $15,000 more."

"You're an asshole, John, a true asshole."

"Name calling just cost you another $5,000 asshole!"

"Man I wish I never met you. I wouldn't have the police breathing down my back and..."

"Look. I don't want to hear it. Just meet me tomorrow at our spot at 2 in the afternoon with my $35,000 and we'll go our separate ways."

Jimmy hung up and called his banker. He agreed to come by for his $40,000 the next day. The extra $5,000 was in case he called John more obscenities.

Janet surprised Mike at the detective bureau. She heard lots of whistles when she entered.

Mike looked up from doing paperwork to see his new friend. He walked over with a big smile. "Hi, Janet, this is a surprise. Let's go into interview room number three where we can talk."

"I brought you a photo of the guy who stole that black Mercedes coupe."

Inside the interview room Janet removed the black and white photograph of John Farran. The photo was somewhat grainy but you could see him sitting in the Mercedes at the tollbooth.

"This is a great help," said Mike.

Six detectives stood in the doorway. Mike handed them the photograph. "One of you make copies and please locate my partner. Guys, this is Janet. Can I get you something to drink?"

"A glass of water would be great."
All 6 detectives dashed for the water cooler.

"We have a face, all we need to do now is put a name with it. Would you like to go for a ride with me? I want to show the photograph to other witnesses."

"Love to," Janet said with a huge smile on her face."

As they started to leave the interview room all 6 detectives approached with little cups of water.

"Gentlemen. I am thirsty but not that thirsty!" laughed Janet taking one of the small cups.

She rode in the front seat of Mike's unmarked police car. Harry was nowhere to be found again.

"I have this partner, Harry Fusco. He's huge, loves to eat all the time. For 8 months now, I have been telling him to let me know when he leaves the office but he always disappears on me."

"I won't disappear on you."

"Good. I can afford to lose a partner but not the woman I want to date."

"Date me! Really?"

"Are you kidding? You're hot, Janet! I look forward to getting to know you better."

Mike pulled up to Kathy's mansion. She was notified by dispatch that the detective was coming. Mike pulled alongside her BMW and exited his car.

"This is the victim of the drive-by shooting that I told you about. I'll introduce you as a police recruit so just play along."

"Ok."

"Good. Make yourself useful and ring the bell please."

Kathy came to the door in tight shorts and an even tighter t-shirt.

At first Kathy didn't see Janet standing to the right of her door when she greeted the detective.

"Hi, Mike, come in. Oh, hello" Kathy made eye contact with Janet.

"Mrs. Sinclair this is police trainee Janet Lee on a ride-along program from the police academy. Can we come in please?"

All 3 sat in her family room that overlooked the huge rock pool and gardens.

"Mrs. Sinclair..." Mike started to say.

"Please call me Kathy."

"Ok, Kathy. I put 6 men in a photo line-up and I need you to look at each photo very carefully. Let us know if the man that robbed your store is here."

Mike showed Kathy the 6 photos. John was photograph number 4. Kathy instantly said, "I'm not sure because he wore a cap and sunglasses but the facial features looks like number 4."

He took the photograph and turned it over. Mike had Kathy sign the back and date it. He put the photo back in place. "Good. Now we just have to put a name to the face and find him."

"Can you tell me where you got that photo?"

"Yes I can. A tollbooth clerk at the airport came up with this photograph. The thief paid his parking toll at her booth after he stole a vehicle from their long-term lot."

"What a lucky break," said Kathy.

"Sure was. We know from the crime lab that your store robbery and drive-by shooting are linked to the same firearm."

Mike looked at his watch. "We have to be going. I have other people to show this photo to."

Kathy walked them to her front door. "Nice to have met you, Janet."

"I sure do like the way your house is decorated."

"Thank you. I love spending my husband's money!"

Kathy called John on his cell but there was no answer. She didn't want to leave him a voice message. She then placed a call to her husband at the store.

"Listen, Jimmy, I'm not coming in anymore. The detective just showed me a photograph of a man that I identified as the one who shot at me. He's driving a stolen vehicle. I know in my heart you are behind all this and..."

"Just wait a minute. I told the detective that I have nothing to do with what's going on."

"I know you are behind all this."

"Listen Kathy. If you recall I was robbed too and also followed. I'm just as much of a victim as you are!"

She just laughed. "Cut the horse shit. My troubles started right after you left my lawyer's office very upset after I turned down your $100,000 offer."

"That's a lot of money for only eleven months of marriage."

"I think you staged your own robbery to give the store money to your hitman as a down payment to kill me. I

132

told this to the detectives and they agreed. When they catch the hitman and he confesses you hired him then I'll be free of you for good." Kathy said before hanging up.

Jimmy called his hitman. "You have to get rid of that Mercedes right now. Kathy identified your photo in a line-up. The police obtained your picture from a tollbooth camera. They know the car is stolen."

"Just keep your cool. I'll dump the car and stay indoors."

John pulled the tarp off his stolen car and departed the area. He dumped the Mercedes in a shopping center parking lot. He rode the bus to the airport and started walking the long-term parking lot.

Mike entered Janet's small but neat apartment. "How long have you lived here?"

"I'm in my 2nd year. I like it because there's plenty of parking downstairs, it's close to work and everyone watches out for each other."

"That's important with crime so high," Mike said as he sat on her leather couch.

"Before I sit do you want something to drink?" asked Janet.

"A beer if you have one."

Janet opened her fridge and pulled out a cold Budweiser. "Bottle or glass?"

"Bottle is great."

Janet handed the cop his brew and sat down next to her crime fighter. "Here's to us," she said with a smile holding her own bottle in the air to toast.

They reviewed the videos of both tollbooths and spotted John twice more. "Can't wait to get my hands on 'Mr. Hot Wheels'," said Mike shutting off the DVD player and moving closer to Janet.

Jimmy left Summit Bank with the money. Steve and his assistant followed him. Both gave him plenty of room when turning on side streets.

A few miles down the road Jimmy spotted a beige Saturn following him. He drove to the mall and sat in his car. He made a call on his cell phone.

"Donna, I need your car. That PI is following me again. Park your car on the west side of the mall by the food court and call me when you arrive."

Jimmy sat in his car and waited. Donna called about 20 minutes later. "I'm here, now what?"

"Leave your car unlocked and the keys under your floor mat. I'll do the same. Take my car and I'll take yours."

Jimmy got out of his car with his briefcase full of cash and pretended to lock it. He entered the mall and made a dash to the west side parking lot to Donna's car. He then drove away.

Steve exited the mall and viewed the Toyota Corolla disappearing around the corner. "Real slick," Steve said to his co-worker who just arrived on foot.

Jimmy called John on his cell phone and confirmed the location and time of the meet. Jimmy was instructed to stop at the Shell Gas Station on State Route 436 and pick up a portable gallon of gas for John who had run out.

He filled up Donna's car first and as instructed bought a gallon of gas from the female clerk who required a $50 deposit.

"A $50 deposit on a gas can," said Jimmy as he paid the clerk.

"Mister, I don't set the prices. I only work here."

Jimmy drove up to John who was leaning against a red Miata. "If the police check my cell phone and see your cell number I am in trouble. They will trace it back to you."

"No need to worry. I took the phone from a tenant's apartment in my apartment complex. He went to China to live with his daughter for a year."

John removed the gas container and briefcase full of money from Jimmy's front seat.

"You have your $35,000 cash now so hand over my gun," Jimmy commanded.

John opened the briefcase, counted the money and reached under his front seat. He came up empty-handed. "I forgot your gun at my place."

"Call me when you are back at your apartment and I'll come for it," said Jimmy. He departed with $5,000 still in his pocket for not calling John any more names.

The hitman waited for Jimmy to drive out of view before starting up the stolen car. He watched the gas gauge climb to full. He placed the full plastic gas container into the bushes and drove off with a smile on his face.

John drove back to his apartment and placed the tarp over his new mode of transportation. He walked over to the manager's door and knocked. There was no answer.

John used a spare key that he had copied earlier when painting apartments in lieu of rent. He opened the door to the old man's office and went to the file cabinet.

Under 'tenants' he found his application and removed it. John relocked the office and entered his own apartment.

Steve and his rookie investigator, Aaron, located Jimmy's car at Donna's store and waited down the street in 2 new and different rental cars.

Jimmy drove back to Donna's business and entered. His girlfriend was helping an elderly woman select a negligee. Donna walked over and whispered in his ear, "She's on her 5th marriage."

Kathy and the real estate agent entered the two story 3 bedroom 2 bath home with a pool located in a middle-income neighborhood.

"This house can be rented monthly for only $900," said Beth.

Kathy walked around the clean and recently painted residence and pulled out her checkbook. "I'll take it."

Kathy handed Beth a check for the first's month's rent and security deposit. She received 2 keys and 2 remote controls for the garage.

"No pets allowed," mentioned Beth walking out the door.

Kathy nodded in agreement, closed the front door and walked into the kitchen. She called John on her cell phone and gave him her new address.

"I found my safe house and the rental furniture will be here at 1 P.M. today."

"Good. Now stay in your mansion tonight and then tomorrow I want you to go into hiding."

"John, the detectives on the case came to my house and showed me 6 photos. I picked your photo based only on facial features and said you had a cap and sunglasses on."

"I'm not worried. If we stick to our plan things will work out. Now tomorrow go into hiding."

Kathy said goodbye and called Detective Anderson. "Mike, I rented that safe house you mentioned I should take. The address is 2445 Pine Lakes Boulevard off of Blank Road.

"Who else knows of this house?"

"The real estate agent, you and my mom are the only ones."

"Good. It's safer that way. I'm in route to show the photo line-up of number 4 to the owners of stolen cars to see if they can ID the thief."

"Can you let me know what they say? Mike."

"Will do. Now lay low until we get to the bottom of this."

John dialed Kathy's number. "I will carry out the 3rd step in our plan tonight. Make sure you are home," John instructed as he drove around in a red Miata compliments of some family traveling to New York City.

Kathy called Steve's travel office and left a message. A few minutes later he called back and said Jimmy was outside the store talking to a young couple pushing a baby stroller.

"Steve, cancel the surveillance. I'll start it again next week. We both know Jimmy is looking for you to follow him."

"I think that's a good idea. Just give me a day's notice if you can, Mrs. Sinclair."

"I will. How much do I owe you?"

"Let's wait until the case is all done."

"Ok."

"I can wait to be paid, Kathy."

"Thanks, Steve. I'll give you as much notice as I can on when to start again."

Kathy stopped at a red box video rental machine and picked up

'Mississippi Burning', with her favorite actor, Gene Hackman. She then drove back to her residence and placed a TV dinner in the oven and opened a bottle of red wine.

THE SNATCH

Jimmy closed his store for the night and was walking to his Honda when John, dressed all in black and wearing gloves surprised him. He poked a gun into Jimmy's ribs. "Get in and open up the passenger door."

Jimmy did as instructed. "Is that my gun?"

"Yep and it's loaded so don't do anything stupid like attract attention."

"Where are we going?" Jimmy asked as he pulled out of Buffalo Bill's parking lot.

"Go to our spot outside of town," demanded John holding a small black bag in his lap. Jimmy now noticed the bag as he drove. "What's in your bag?"

"Liquor for our own little party. We need to talk. Now shut up and drive."

Thirty minutes later Jimmy pulled into the spot he had met John at earlier in the day.

"Cut the engine and turn off the car lights."

Jimmy did as instructed. John unzipped his bag and pulled out a full bottle of Jim Beam whiskey. He opened it and said, "Drink it."

Jimmy started to complain but was cut short by a sudden thrust of the gun into his rib cage.

"I said no talking just drink."

Jimmy drank slowly.

"Hurry it up."

Jimmy drank faster and after 10 minutes had about 30% of the bottle finished.

"I can't drink anymore."

Jimmy didn't see the butt of his gun coming down on his head but did feel the pain as the weapon made contact. He was knocked out cold.

John went into the bushes by the side of the road and retrieved the can of gas that Jimmy had bought earlier.

The hitman slid his partner in crime over to the passenger side then got behind the wheel and drove away.

Thirty minutes later John pulled into Kathy's driveway. John poured gasoline around the foundation of the house, lit a match, and quickly backed the car out of the driveway.

Kathy watched John set the fire. She followed their plan and dialed 911. Kathy screamed her situation to the operator that answered.

"Come quickly to my house. It is on fire. I saw my husband's car backing out of the driveway!"

She gave her address to the operator and calmly walked out the back door of her home dressed only in a nightgown.

John drove a few blocks, turned right and crashed the Honda into some parked cars. He quickly pulled Jimmy, who was still passed out, behind the wheel of his damaged car.

John quickly poured the rest of the whiskey on his partner in crime, wiped the bottle of his prints and vanished into the darkness.

Mike arrived shortly after the Tupelo Fire Department put out the small fire.

He located Kathy on the porch of a neighbor. She was wrapped in a blanket and surrounded by police and fire personnel.

"Mrs. Sinclair are you alright?"

"No, I'm not. Jimmy did this. I saw his car backing out of our driveway. I then spotted the flames. Thank God I took a break from watching a movie to go to the bathroom."

"Where in the house were you?"

"I stay in the upstairs guest bedroom in the back of the house. Jimmy has the master."

"You sure it was his car you saw?"

"Yes!"

"How do you know it was his car?"

"He is having exhaust and oil leak problems. There were puffs of smoke coming from the car as it backed out of the driveway."

Mike's answered his cell phone. He listened and then spoke. "Hold him at the scene. I'll be right over."

Mike turned to Kathy and said, "Your husband crashed his car a few blocks from here. He appears to be drunk.

The officers on the scene say there are an empty whiskey bottle and a container of gas on the floorboard."

The Fire Marshal approached. "Mike, Ma'am, the fire is out. Very little damage, mostly exterior, definitely arson."

"Thanks, Chief. Get me your full report as soon as you can."

"Will do, Detective."

Mike turned to a uniformed officer. "Take Mrs. Sinclair to wherever she wants to go."

He turned back to Kathy. "Mrs. Sinclair, this officer will give you a ride to another location. Please call me in the morning so I can take your full statement."

"I'll stay at my mother's. She is waiting up for me now."

"May I please have a phone number where I can reach you?" asked Mike.

Kathy gave him her mother's phone number. She watched Mike walk back to his car and drive away.

The detective pulled up to the crash site. He observed Jimmy being attended to by the medics.

Mike smelled the strong odor of alcohol on the store owner. He inspected the damaged Honda and observed the empty liquor bottle and gas container on the floorboard.

Mike walked over to a uniformed officer. "Make sure the crime lab photographs the empty liquor bottle and gas container, dusts the items for finger prints and have the medic draw blood for DUI."

"Yes, Sir," the officer responded.

Mike asked the medic a few questions. "Which hospital are you taking him to?"

"County General."

"How bad is he?"

"Mostly bruises but he does have a bump on the back of his head."

Mike walked over to the same policeman. "Charge him with attempted murder and arson. Keep an officer with him at the hospital."

"Will do."

"Good, I'm going back to bed." He walked to his vehicle and drove away.

It only took 20 minutes for John to arrive back at Buffalo Bill's. He entered his stolen Miata and drove by the accident scene. A tow truck was hooking up Jimmy's damaged car. John laughed as he drove away.

The police car arrived at a condo complex. Carol was standing out front waiting for her daughter. As Kathy exited the vehicle her mother said, "I never did like Jimmy."

"Please don't worry, Mom. He won't be my husband much longer. Can you make us some hot cocoa like you always did when I was younger?"

Carol led her daughter into the elevator and spoke as the doors closed. "Cocoa you want, cocoa you get."

Steve received a call from Kathy. "Jimmy's just been arrested for attempted murder and arson."

"What? When?"

"Early this morning. He tried to burn down my house with me in it."

"Are you okay?"

"Yes. It was bad timing on my part in taking you off of following my husband."

"What now?"

"I need to restart the surveillance on him. Please pick Jimmy back up if and when he bonds out. I definitely need to know where Jimmy will be at all times."

"I'll call the jail and ask them to notify me when he is bonding out."

"Thanks, Steve."

"No problem, Kathy. Call if you need anything. Just try to rest."

"Steve, talking of rest, call me in a few days about some upcoming cruises. I sure do need one."

"I know of one right now. I'm holding the brochure as we speak. It's a 14-day singles cruise from Miami to the Virgin Islands."

"Perfect, I'll come over in a few days and buy my ticket." Kathy sat down next to her mom and slowly sipped on her hot cup of cocoa smiling as she did so.

The next morning Kathy drove to the police station. She had an appointment with the detectives regarding her side of the arson incident.

Mike was not available but surprisingly Harry was. They both went into interview room 4.

"Where's Mike?" inquired Kathy.

"My partner's teaching out at the police academy. Mike said to tell you he would try his best to be back before we are finished."

"What topic is he teaching the recruits?"

"Interview techniques." Harry handed Kathy a pad, pen and instructed her to write what occurred from the time she was in her bedroom until the fire department arrived.

"Care for anything to drink while you write?"

"A diet coke would be good."

Five minutes later Harry was back with the diet soda and Kathy was done with her statement.

Harry read the whole thing. "Are you positive it was Jimmy's old car backing out of your driveway? There are many white Hondas in this town."

"I am positive. I even underlined the word *positive* in my statement."

"I see that."

"Jimmy's car has recently developed an exhaust problem so when you floor the gas pedal white smoke comes out and that is what I saw under the street lights," Kathy restated emphatically.

"You will make a great witness Mrs. Sinclair."

"Really! Why?"

"You come across as an honest woman," Harry soothed. "Off the record may I ask you a very personal question?"

"You can ask but I might not answer," came Kathy's guarded response.

Harry sat down with his own diet soda and asked, "What went wrong in your marriage? According to the store customers you both were lovebirds and did everything together."

"When Jimmy and I first started dating he worked an awful lot of hours. He didn't hire the help he needed to give himself a normal social life. I convinced Jimmy to slow down so we could spend more time together."

Kathy took a deep breath and continued to satisfy Harry's curiosity. "Then once we got married he went back to his old workaholic ways. I was lonely. I sent for my mother, bought her a small condo and spent my spare time with her."

"Too many men neglect their woman. I know I did."

"When he came home there was no romance. I suspected another woman. I confronted him one day and he admitted he was having an affair. He said he didn't love me anymore and wanted a divorce," lied Kathy.

As she became more agitated the detective began to regret he had asked the question. Kathy wasn't finished yet.

"We started fighting all the time so I moved to the guest room. I thought if I got an attorney Jimmy would refocus his attention towards me instead of the store. I was wrong."

"I'm sorry to hear that Mrs. Sinclair," interrupted Harry having heard enough.

Kathy rattled on, "My lawyer says I am entitled to about $4 million. I would take much less and move on but Jimmy has been treating me like dirt! I decided to stay and fight and take as much as I can get. Jimmy calls me a gold digger so I might as well not disappoint him!"

"I think you are doing the right thing Mrs. Sinclair," Harry interjected. "I was married once too. Abby and I were together for 19 years and we have 2 beautiful boys. Believe it or not, at one point, I was in tip-top shape but after the divorce I let myself go."

Harry continued to reminisce. "I drank like crazy for a few years and spent my savings on wild women and alcohol. My sons got me back on the right path."

"Do you live with them now?"

"No. I live in a double wide trailer outside of town. By the way, I am actively seeking a female companion in case you know of any nice single women," Harry said.

"I am happy to hear you are doing better. I will keep my eyes open for you. I know of many single store customers. Exactly what type of woman are you attracted to?"

"I'm 53 years old. I am 5'8" and weigh about 240 pounds. My ideal woman would be about 50 years old and must love to cook because I love to eat!"

Kathy took the last swallow of her diet soda as Mike walked in. "Sorry, I'm late."

Harry handed Kathy's statement to his partner. Mike quickly read the 3 pages. "This will do."

He handed the legal pad back to Harry and turned to Kathy. "Would you like another soda?" he asked as he took a seat at the long interview table.

"No thanks."

All 3 continued making small talk.

John drove over to the town of Starkville located about 70 miles from Tupelo. He pulled up to Comcar Truck Sales. John approached a guard.

"I'm about to buy a new rig. Can I walk the yard and take a look at all your new trucks?"

"Be my guest. Need a flashlight?" the friendly sentry asked offering him a small flashlight.

"I'll take you up on your offer, and thanks."

Jimmy was led into interrogation room 3 by a uniformed officer. Mike walked in alone with a notepad, tape recorder and 2 cups of hot coffee.

"I don't want any coffee."

Mike sighed, "I didn't ask if you wanted any coffee. Both cups are for me since we'll be here awhile. I'm going to turn the recorder on and read you your rights."

"I know my rights. I'm innocent of all charges whatever they are."

"Good. I'll read them anyway."

After Mike went into his standard rhetoric 'You have the right to a lawyer Miranda rights', He asked Jimmy why he tried to burn his own house down with his wife in it.

"I didn't try to burn my house down."

"You didn't? Then why were you found drunk behind the wheel of your crashed car with an empty gas can only 4 blocks away?"

"Coincidence."

"Don't make me laugh." Mike replied.

"It is true."

"We received a phone tip on where you bought the gas and which clerk sold you the gas can. The employee identified you from that observation room right there," pointed Mike at the mirror to his left.

"The clerk even remembers you making a comment about the $50 deposit. It's her station's gas can too because their label was found on the bottom of the can sold. So why would you need a can of gas unless it's to burn down your house with your wife in bed?"

"I bought gas for a motorist who flagged me down. When I got back the motorist was gone."

"Why not just return to the gas station and get your $50.00 deposit back?"

"I had to get back to the grocery store. I thought I would send Billy, our clerk, back for the refund."

"Why didn't you?" questioned the detective.

"I got busy and forgot," Jimmy said laying his head into his hands.

"Did you hire anyone to do your wife harm?"

"No. I plan to just get a divorce and move on."

"Really!"

"It's true."

"What about the phony deposit robbery over at Summit Bank?"

"What phony robbery? You said you have a witness who saw a gun."

"Yes, and the witness says you just handed over your 2 money bags to the robber who held out his empty hands - no gun in sight. The witness said that when she came over to offer help you were as calm as could be, yet you told me you were scared."

"She's mistaken. I was scared."

154

"You knew we had a rash of store robberies yet you failed to inform your wife to be careful."

"I thought I told her."

"How did the robber know to enter via the unlocked storage room back door?"

"Maybe he walked in through the front door without being seen."

"Are you willing to take a polygraph? Mr. Sinclair."

"How does that machine work?"

"We attach instruments that monitor heartbeat, breathing and perspiration based on your answers to questions like, 'Have you hired anyone to do harm to you wife'?"

"I think I'll decline the polygraph test at this time."

"I'm going to put you back in your cell as I have a search warrant for your residence."

"Search warrant? There's nothing to find at my house!"

"Well, Mr. Sinclair, the city pays me pretty good to do my job and I'm following basic routine investigative procedures."

"You do not need a search warrant. I will gladly give you my okay."

Jimmy was led back to his cell and was allowed to make one phone call.

Donna picked up her business line and was happy to hear her lover's voice.

"Can you come visit me? Hours are 6 to 9 every night."

"I'll be there tonight. Want me to bring you anything?"

"Yes, Donna, wear that green top with Dallas on the front and bring me a USA Today newspaper."

"Anything you want. Dallas will see you in about 5 hours – love you," Donna said as she hung up.

Jimmy entered his small cell which was occupied by a thin, black male with bad breath. "Want to play a game of checkers?" said his cell mate.

"Nope. I just want to relax till my old lady visits me in 5 hours," he said as he climbed into his bunk.

As the jail guard locked their cell door he warned Jimmy. "Watch out! Leroy cheats."

Donna sat on a visitor's stool dressed to kill with her hair in a ponytail, wearing extra perfume, which all the guards noticed. In her hand was the latest edition of the 'USA Today'. Jimmy's favorite newspaper.

The guards told Donna she could show the newspaper to her man through the thick glass that separated the free people from the not so free. They assured her they would drop it off at his cell later.

Jimmy walked in with a sad look on his face but smiled when he saw his future wife. "Thanks for coming, Donna. I missed you."

"I missed you too, Baby." She shows her man the newspaper and says, "The guards will bring it to your room later."

"It's called a cell, Honey, not a room."

"I know but room sounds better to me. What do you do in your room to pass the time?"

"I think of you and lose at checkers to a black man."

"Guess who came in and bought a black nightie today?"

"I don't know. Who?"

"Kathy," Donna gushed.

"What?"

"Yes! I was as shocked as you are now."

"Tell me more."

"We just made small talk. I don't think she knows I'm the future Mrs. Sinclair. She tried it on in the shop and has a really firm body."

"Well don't worry, Donna. She's cold as ice in bed at least with me."

"What's going to happen to you tomorrow?" asked Donna.

"I will post bond and then we will go to breakfast. I'm dying for some hotcakes."

Jimmy took a deep breath. "Donna, I need you to be strong while I deal with my situation. I know now I should never have hired someone to kill Kathy."

"That is what divorce is for, Baby."

"I was just so angry when I realized that I was a sucker to marry the woman who turned out to be a real gold digger."

"Your parents warned you about her."

"Yes they did. I should have listened to them."

"If you had listen to your parents you would be a free man right now."

"Every time I saw Kathy spending my money on things like: her BMW convertible, jewelry, her mom's condo, or talking about cruises and other trips, I just got madder."

Jimmy concluded, "I work very hard down at Buffalo Bill's. I drive an old white Honda. I just felt trapped."

"Jimmy, I know it is bad timing to say this but you really make me mad – doing something so stupid like hiring a hitman!"

He nodded his head up and down in agreement.

Donna fumed. "All you had to do was open your wallet, give her some money and she'd be out of your life."

"I wish I did."

"You and I could work real hard to earn that money back. Now you face possible jail time, you have to hire an expensive lawyer – but most of all we are separated by metal bars and for how long?"

"Sweet Pea, I know it's a mess but I'll figure a way out of it. Soon you will be Mrs. Jimmy Sinclair."

Donna was walking to her car in the parking lot when the 2 detectives pulled up in their unmarked vehicle. She walked over and squatted down.

"Hello, Miss Johnson," said Mike with a friendly smile that Donna thought was phony. "Visiting anyone we know?"

"You 2 have the wrong man locked up. My Jimmy wouldn't hurt anyone," vowed the loyal Donna.

"You may be right but we are looking for the hitman we believe, 'My Jimmy', hired," said Mike.

"Jimmy isn't the type of man who would do that. He would just divorce and move on."

"You sure about that?" asked Harry eating a small bag of pretzels. "We know Jimmy drinks a little. We have the bartender's statement from The Hide-Away Bar and we all know what liquor can do."

"Around me he doesn't drink so I wouldn't know," said Donna.

"The bond hearing is at 9 tomorrow. If Jimmy bonds out my advice is for him to stay way away from his wife," Mike warned.

"What do you mean *if*?" asked Donna.

"Bond hearings can go either way. The judge has to think of the victim's safety and the seriousness of the charges," Mike said as Harry nodded his head in agreement.

Donna said thanks for the bond information and slowly walked away.

Mike and Harry arranged to see Jimmy in an interview room and waited for him to enter.

"Too bad we didn't find any evidence at his house or in his car," said Harry.

Jimmy entered the interview room and the guard removed his handcuffs. The guard assured the detectives he would be right outside their door.

"Jimmy, we saw Donna in the parking lot. We told her to tell you, if and when you bond out, to stay as far away from your wife," warned Mike.

Harry nodded in agreement as he ate a candy bar.

"There's no *if*. I'll bond out and believe me, I don't ever want to see my wife again," said Jimmy.

"We searched your wrecked car and are releasing it from the tow yard. You can get it fixed now," said Harry placing a release form in front of Jimmy to sign.

He signed the paper and looked at both detectives. "You didn't find anything in your search of my house did you?"

Harry spoke next. "Not saying. We will see you at the bond hearing."

The detectives left the interview room and the guard escorted Jimmy back to his cell. "Could I get a snack?" he asked nicely.

"Sure," laughed the guard not stopping until Jimmy was securely locked up in his cell on the 2nd floor of the east wing.

The next morning Jimmy was escorted by the bailiff into the courtroom. He smiled at Donna and sat down on a special bench for prisoners.

Twenty minutes went by before Jimmy stood in front of Judge Vicky Trustmark.

The judge listened to the State Attorney's side of the story and turned to Jimmy, "If you can't afford an attorney the court can appoint one for you free of charge."

"I can afford an attorney but I wanted to stand before you Judge and plead my case. May I speak?"

"Go ahead," the judge assented.

"I've lived in this community all my life. I own Buffalo Bill's Grocery Store and have never been in trouble with the law - not even a speeding ticket. I promise that if I am let out on bail I will move out of my house and into a motel. I will avoid having any contact with my wife."

"Very well Mr. Sinclair I'll grant you bail but do obtain a lawyer. These charges are serious and if convicted

you will spend a great deal of time in
the state penitentiary."

"Thank you, Judge. I will seek
counsel once I'm released."

THE TRAP

Jimmy exited the front entrance of the Tupelo jail and kissed Donna. He stopped on the sidewalk to take in his freedom.

"Feels good to be free. I plan to go over to the store and tell Kathy the truth. I did hire a man to kill her, that I changed my mind, paid the guy off and that I'll give her what she wants in the divorce so I can start my new life with you, Baby."

Donna and Jimmy kissed again while Steve videoed the whole romantic episode.

Jimmy pulled up to Donna's apartment. He got out and opened her passenger door. "I'll borrow your car, meet Kathy and come back home as quickly as I can."

"Why can't I come with you?" Donna complained.

"It's my problem. I started it so I'll finish it. Besides, I want Kathy in a good mood and seeing you next to me might upset her. My lawyer said there is a possibility charges can be reduced or dismissed but to do so I need her cooperation. I want Kathy *so* happy that she drops the charges. Just

stay home Sweetie and get 2 cups of tea
ready. I'll be back soon."

"Ok. Don't upset her."

"I will keep her happy."

Jimmy kissed Donna goodbye and
departed the neighborhood. He was
followed by Steve and his helper,
Aaron, in their rental cars.

Steve called Kathy and gave her an
update on what her spouse was doing.

"Thanks, Steve. I'm so afraid of
him. Now I hope to avoid him."

Kathy then called John and they
talked for a few minutes.

Mike and Harry pulled up to the
residence of Robert Wheeler. They
knocked and showed their badges to Mrs.
Wheeler who answered the door.

They were led to the master
bedroom where Mr. Wheeler was resting.
Both of his legs were in thigh-high
casts.

"Hello, Sir. I am Detective Mike
Anderson and this is my partner Harry
Fusco. Like I mentioned to you on the
telephone we have a suspect in the
theft of your car."

Mike continued, "His method is to
chat up a family to find out how long
they will be away. Once they depart on
their flight he steals their car. I
have a set of 6 photos and I need you

166

to view each one closely and pick out the man who chatted you up before your flight."

"Take your time," said Harry.

Mr. Wheeler surveyed all the photos and stopped at number 4. "This is the man. He seemed like a nice guy too."

Mike handed the man his ink pen. "Can you please sign your name below the photo and date it? That will show that number 4 was your choice." Mike retrieved his pen and photo line-up sheet after the man did as instructed.

Harry had to ask, "What happened to you?"

"I was rock climbing in Utah and fell 20 feet. Both of my legs and ankles are shattered."

"Bad luck," mumbled Harry. His ears perked up when Mrs. Wheeler entered the room and asked, "Would you 2 officers care for a piece of homemade pumpkin pie?"

Mike indicated that he didn't care for any, but Harry, true to form didn't refuse the offer.

"Would it be possible to take the pies to go? We have more people we have to interview," Harry stated after receiving a cross look from his partner.

A few minutes later Mrs. Wheeler walked outside and gave Harry a plastic bag. "Here you go, Gentlemen."

Harry gratefully took his next meal from the lady. Once inside their vehicle he reached for his slice.

"Always eating. You might as well have my piece too," sighed Mike.

"Thanks, Partner!" said Harry as he took his first large bite.

Jimmy went to his grocery store and saw Billy working behind the counter. "Where's Kathy?"

"She said she wasn't coming in here anymore."

Jimmy walked back to Donna's car and left for his home. He drove to his residence but didn't find any cars in the driveway or in the garage.

Jimmy walked through his 5,000 square foot home, checked the game room, kitchen, pool area and then walked into the master bedroom.

Kathy's clothes were gone from her open closet. Jimmy checked her dresser drawers and they were empty too.

He turned to leave the bedroom when John suddenly appeared in the doorway blocking Jimmy's exit from the room.

"Kathy moved out. She's afraid of you."

Jimmy noticed John putting black gloves on. "What's with the gloves? I paid you off," Jimmy exclaimed.

"I know you paid me off but I got to thinking – why be 6 of 7 when I can be 7 for 7 and keep my perfect hit record."

"You're an ass," Jimmy said as he followed John toward the front door.

"I followed Kathy the other day to her new place and I am going there now to be 7 for 7." repeated John.

He ran out the front door to his stolen car and drove off, making sure not to lose Jimmy who was trying to catch up.

The 2 private investigators followed both men out of the area. The trap was set and soon Kathy would be free of her husband whom she never did love.

Kathy sipped her hot cup of tea and waited upstairs with the loaded 45 automatic she borrowed from her mom.

As Kathy waited she thought back on how she tricked Jimmy into marrying her.

She saw a photo of Jimmy and his parents in the local paper about 18 months ago. The article discussed the history of Buffalo Bill's and showed a photo of Jimmy and his parents.

Kathy visited the store to see if Jimmy was as handsome in person as the photo depicted. Kathy stood in line and noticed no ring on his finger.

She introduced herself and inquired about the 'Help Wanted' sign in the window.

"We need a part-time cashier from 5 P.M. to closing."

"I can start today," said Kathy.

Jimmy asked, "Do you have any cashier experience?"

"Yes. I worked for Burger King and a clothing store while I attended college," lied Kathy.

Jimmy handed her an application from below the counter. She quickly completed the form and handed it back in.

Jimmy looked it over and said, "You can start tomorrow at 5 P.M. I will pay you $10 an hour to start."

Kathy thanked Jimmy and walked out vowing to marry the rich man. No way was she going to live in a rundown trailer all her life. She did not want to return to muggy LaBelle, Florida, or move back in with her mom and sisters.

While riding the Greyhound bus out of LaBelle she promised not to return until she was married to a rich and successful man. Kathy kept her one-way Greyhound ticket in her purse as a reminder.

She read how rich men worried about marrying gold diggers that only wanted their money.

Kathy wanted to marry a rich man but would not show she was a gold digger till she was married.

She told herself not to accept anything a rich man offered her while dating or later when engaged. Once married there would be plenty of time to spend his money.

She checked the laws in Mississippi regarding divorce and liked what she read.

At first, Jimmy worked too many hours in the store but Kathy changed that little by little. She got him to hire stock clerks and cashiers so they could go out.

Jimmy bought her jewelry but Kathy always made him return it. She would tug on his hair when she kissed him saying, "I don't want jewelry, Honey, just you."

Every time Jimmy tried to buy her clothes, shop for a new car, or take her to expensive restaurants, Kathy would make him take it back or refuse to go out. It worked because 6 months later they were married.

The first thing the gold digger did was to move her mom out of that trailer in LaBelle, Florida, to a nice, one bedroom condo in Tupelo, a few miles from her mansion.

She also spent Jimmy's money by buying her mom a new car and opening a savings account with $20,000. She then hired an interior decorator to redo the condo and the mansion.

Kathy knew her mother couldn't believe her stroke of luck. From a trailer, no car, or money in LaBelle, Florida to a beautiful condo, a new car, clothes, and money in the bank in Tupelo.

Carol thought her daughter was happy and was shocked when Kathy finally told her the truth.

"Mom, I married Jimmy only for his money. I did it for us. I was tired of being poor."

Kathy purchased her new, green BMW convertible and was looking for a way to end her marriage without a long, drawn out court battle, when John, the hitman, fatefully knocked on her door.

Her thoughts were interrupted when Kathy's phone rang.

"I'll be there in 2 minutes. Be ready - got Jimmy following close behind."

Kathy picked up her 45 automatic and replied, "I'll be waiting in the master bedroom. Come upstairs to the first door on the right."

John put down his cell phone and turned left onto Kathy's street.

He pulled up quickly to the 2-story colonial rental house and stopped right behind Kathy's BMW.

John opened the unlocked front door and ran up the stairs to the only lit room in the house.

Jimmy was yelling, "He's got a gun!" as he ran into the bedroom right behind John.

There stood Kathy waiting with a 45 automatic in her hand. "Drop the gun now," she commanded.

John did as instructed.

"Both of you get on the ground, spread out your hands and feet and do it now!" shouted Kathy waving her gun around.

Jimmy followed her orders.

Kathy kicked Jimmy's gun towards the far wall. Her husband started to speak, "Kathy, I tried to warn . . ."

"Shut up, Jimmy, just shut up."

Kathy dialed 911 on her cell phone. The operator asked if this was an emergency.

She replied in a very nervous voice, "I'm holding at gunpoint 2 armed men at 2445 Pine Lakes Boulevard, upstairs, first bedroom to the right. My name is Kathy Sinclair. Send help."

Steve started reviewing the video but the battery on his camera died.

He tried calling Kathy's phone, but got her voice mail. "Kathy, it's me, Steve. I'm outside your place. Are you alright? Call me back."

The PI and his helper both heard sirens. Aaron picked up his own video camera and videoed the action as police cars came screaming down the street with their sirens and lights.

Three officers rushed to the front door with their guns drawn. "Police – it's the police!" one of the officers yelled.

"I'm up here. I called you. I'm Kathy Sinclair," she shouted. "I'm holding two men at gunpoint, first room on the right at the top of the stairs,"

"OK, Ma'am, take it easy. We are slowly coming up."

The officers cautiously walked up the stairs and one officer peeked around the corner before pointing his gun into the room.

"Ma'am, place your gun slowly on the bed and keep your hands up."

Kathy did as she was told. The officers entered the bedroom and picked up both guns.

They handcuffed John and Jimmy and marched them downstairs. She asked the officers to get in touch with detective Anderson who was looking for both men.

The first officer to enter the room asked Kathy to start from the beginning.

"Detective Mike Anderson arrested my husband, soon-to-be-ex, the other day and charged him with attempted murder."

The officer started writing down on his notepad what the victim was telling him.

"The detective told me he suspected my husband of hiring a hitman, the guy in the gray shirt you just removed from my room. The detective told me for my safety I should move out of my own residence to a safe house until he caught the hitman, which is what I did, so how did they find me?"

"I don't know Ma'am. The 38 on the floor - who was carrying that?"

"My husband," lied Kathy. "I heard footsteps running up the stairs and the 2 men came dashing in and I just picked up my gun and pointed it at them both."

An officer entered the room and said, "Detective Anderson is on the way, ETA about 10 minutes."

Aaron walked over and videoed Jimmy and John sitting in the back of 2 different police cars.

Mike arrived quickly and was directed upstairs to the crime scene. He entered the bedroom and saw Kathy talking to a uniformed officer.

"Some safe house I found," Kathy said.

"Who knew about this address?" Mike asked.

"My Mom, the Real Estate Agent, and You," she lied.

"When I interview them I will find out how they located your safe house."

Kathy just nodded her head.

"How about tomorrow you come to the station and I take your official statement since right now you must be emotionally drained?"

176

"I am drained, lied Kathy. Can I go back to my own home now?"

"Why not? Both of these men won't be going anywhere."

An officer interrupted their conversation by handing detective Anderson a note.

Mike read the message and then placed the note into his pocket. "Kathy, I have to go. Call me in the morning so I can take your statement."

He then departed the area.

Mike called the Tupelo Airport Auto Theft Bureau. The message was about the Mercedes Benz coupe.

"Hey, Mike, this is Detective Thomson. You wanted to be notified if a certain Mercedes Benz coupe was recovered."

"Yes?" Mike replied as he waited in anticipation for some good news.

"The vehicle is registered to Jay and Julie Hopkins. We located the vehicle at the Airport Hilton by the pool parking lot. We are processing it now. Any instructions for us?"

"Just send the heart medication in the glove box to the victims. They seemed to really need it. Send me a copy of the report as well. One more thing, I arrested a man tonight named John Farran and he was driving a red

Miata. My guess is he stole it from your long-term parking lot."

"We'll check our customer list and I will mail out the medication."

Mike normally would have sped to the Airport to ascertain more details but he had cancelled on Janet before and wasn't about to do it again.

She was waiting with his favorite chicken teriyaki. A few hours later he left with Janet waving goodbye.

On the front seat of his police vehicle was a generous hot plate of leftovers for Harry compliments of Janet.

Mike entered interrogation room number 1 and sat across from John who had an arm handcuffed to a wall mount.

"Let me read you your rights."

"Detective, save your breath. I know my rights and I want a lawyer," John snarled.

Mike left the room and walked into interrogation room number 2. There sat Jimmy, handcuffed.

"Before we get started would you like anything, Jimmy?"

"The *USA Today*," Jimmy replied.

"When you are back in your cell I'll have one brought to you. Let me read you your rights again."

"I want a lawyer right now. I know my rights," Jimmy replied.

Mike left the store owner and walked into the observation room where his partner was eating Janet's dinner.

"Two for 2, Mike?" grinned Harry with sauce dripping from his chin.

"Yep. They can have their lawyers. With Kathy as a witness and a gun recovered I think we have a strong case."

"I agree," said his partner.

John was escorted by a jail guard to a phone. He called a criminal defense lawyer recommended by Kathy.

Attorney Joseph McKinsey advised John not to say a word and reassured him he would be down there shortly.

John walked back to his cell, stopping briefly in front of Jimmy's cell. "Room service. How do you take your coffee?"

Jimmy looked up from reading the 'USA Today' to reply, "You are one crazy asshole."

"That will cost you $5,000." John kept laughing as he was led back to his cell. He was laying in his bunk trying to take a nap when rookie police officer Hanagan stopped in front of his cell.

"Well. I finally meet Mr. Hot Wheels."

John lifted his head from his upper bunk. "Who are you?"

"I am the officer who stopped you in front of the house where you hid the van in the garage," Hanagan beamed proudly.

"You have to admit it worked - I got away."

"Yes you did and because you were so clever I brought you a small gift to remember the incident by."

The officer tossed John a key chain through the bars. Attached was a Hot Wheels car. "I am nicknaming you 'Mr. Hot Wheels'."

John looked at the cool little sports car and said, "Thanks for the gift."

Kathy entered the detective bureau and was placed in interview room number 1. Mike walked in with a large, yellow notepad.

"Hi, Kathy."

"Hello, Mike," she responded.

"We have to do this interview by the book. That's why you're in this

room instead of at my desk. Here is a
notepad and pen."

Kathy takes the items.

"While I'm gone, please write down
all that happened from the time the 2
men entered your house until the police
arrived. I'll be back soon."

"Glad we finally have them under
arrest," said Kathy.

"Me too. I have to sit in on an
interview with the hitman's lawyer."

Mike walked into interview room 3
and was introduced to attorney Joseph
McKinsey sitting next to John.

"My client has an offer on the
table."

"What is your offer?"

"You drop attempted murder and
grand theft auto charges for his full
cooperation against Jimmy Sinclair."

"No way. We have a strong case,"
asserted Mike.

"Do you? I really don't think so.
According to the arresting officer's
report the victim can't put any weapon
in my client's hand."

"I will ask the victim if that is
true."

"My client will testify that Jimmy
Sinclair asked him to go along for a

ride. That he didn't know what Jimmy
was going to do before he did it."

"Horseshit. What about all the
grand theft auto charges we just filed?
We have videos of him at the toll
booths exiting the airport, plus all
the owners will testify that Jimmy took
their cars."

"As you say, *horseshit*. My client
is on videos in cars that the owners
asked *him* to drive. We will say that
one owner asked him to pick up the
heart medication his wife needed at
their house and we'll claim in court
the old man is senile."

"We have the latest stolen car at
the victim's safe house."

"Now we know Detective that 1 bird
in the hand is better than 2 birds in a
bush."

"True."

"So Detective, let my client walk
from all charges and we'll help you
nail the husband for attempted murder."

"I don't think so. We have a
strong case," said Harry eating a
cookie.

"Do you really want my client for
auto theft or Jimmy Sinclair for
attempted murder?"

"We have the victim in the next
room. Let my partner talk to her."

Mike left the room and went to see Kathy who just finished her written statement.

After he finished reading it he asked, "Are you willing to testify it was your husband holding the gun when he barged into your bedroom?"

"Yes. I need Jimmy off the street and behind bars or my life will always be in danger."

"In the other room I have the attorney for John Farran. He wants to make a deal that allows us to nail your husband for attempted murder but allow his accomplice to walk free."

"Fine by me. I need all the help I can get. I know Jimmy will hire the best and most expensive attorney in town."

"Go home and I'll let you know what we decide to do," said Mike.

He received a call from the lab right after exiting the interview room.

The gun recovered at the safe house belonged to Jimmy Sinclair and the slugs from the store and residence walls matched his 38 pistol.

In the hallway Harry called the Mississippi State Attorney on duty. Mike walked up and listened in.

"We have 2 men in custody. Both are charged with attempted murder. One is the husband of the victim and the other is the hitman he hired. The lawyer for the hitman wants to make a deal."

"What is the deal, Detective?"

"His client will tell us everything in return for immunity."

State Attorney Dicenso asked, "How strong is your evidence on the hitman?"

"Not too strong, Sir. The victim tells us her husband entered the safe house holding a gun. The hitman claims he tried to prevent the husband from killing his wife."

"What else does the man say?"

"That the husband paid him money to kill his wife. To tell you the truth I really want to nail the husband."

"Then give the man immunity if it helps you nail the husband."

Harry and Mike were happy. They had the okay from the State Attorney to make the deal to nail Jimmy.

Attorney McKinsey stood up when Mike and his partner walked in.

"Attorney McKinsey. We're willing along with State Attorney Dicenso to drop all charges as long as your client is 100% honest and cooperates from this moment on."

"Fine. Turn the recorder on please and put what you just told me on tape. My client will cooperate fully," the attorney directed.

Harry ate another cookie while his partner asked John questions.

"How did Jimmy Sinclair hire you?"

"We were in The Hide-Away Bar as customers. We started talking about his wife. He mentioned she was a gold digger and that she fooled him into marrying her. He said she married him for his money. Jimmy wanted out of this sham of a relationship and was willing to pay someone to do it."

"How much did he offer to pay you for killing his wife?"

"Jimmy told me to meet him at Summit Bank. He handed over 2 bank deposit bags with $15,000 in cash. In one of the bags was his 38 revolver. He was going to give me an additional $15,000 after the killing."

"What else did you 2 discuss?"

"I asked if he wanted her shot in the head or torso and he said the torso. He showed me the newspaper article with the robberies of the store owners. He thought it would be a good idea to make it look like a robbery. Jimmy wrote down his wife's store hours on a piece of paper which is in my wallet."

Mike turned to his partner, "Go to property. Bring me his wallet please."

Harry left the interview room.

Mike turned to John. "Tell me about the store robbery."

"Jimmy called me on my cell phone and said he left the back door unlocked."

"What else did he say and do?"

"He told me what time that day to come by since he wouldn't be there. I came in the back door but I never had any intention of hurting anyone."

Mike checked his tape recorder to make sure it was on and working.

"My first plan was to take his hit deposit and run. Then I visited the grocery store and saw how pretty his wife was. I knew if I left town Jimmy would just find someone else to kill her."

"How mad was Jimmy about being tricked into this sham of a marriage?" asked Mike.

"He was very pissed off that she tricked him into marrying her. So my idea was to purposely miss shooting her but make it look like I tried."

"Is that why the bullets we located in the wall were at the 11 foot mark?"

"Yes. I did the same thing at the drive-by shooting at her house."

"How did you know his wife was outside? Were you watching her?"

"No. Jimmy called me and said he was leaving his house and that his wife was putting on gardening gloves."

"So you went over to his house and did what?"

"When I got there I just aimed real high and drove off in Jimmy's Honda which he loaned me."

"What was Jimmy's reaction to your second failed attempt at killing his wife?"

"He was very mad - asked me what kind of a hitman I was and said that his wife was lucky - so lucky she should go to Vegas."

"Then what happened?"

"I told Jimmy I didn't want to go on with this killer-for-hire thing."

"What did he say?"

"He offered me more money to continue."

"How much more?"

"$35,000 cash."

"Where is all this money now?"

"It's hidden in my apartment under my dresser, mixed in with my own $15,000."

"Why under your dresser instead of in a bank?"

"I grew up in a family that didn't trust banks."

Harry entered the room and gave John's billfold to his partner. Mike looked inside the leather wallet. Kathy's work schedule was tucked inside the billfold in what appeared to be in Jimmy's handwriting.

"Now, Partner, go to John's apartment with a Lab Tech. Take photos and document the cash under the dresser that Jimmy gave John to kill his wife."

Mike wrote down the address and turned back to John and said, "What did you and Jimmy do next?"

"We met at the Hide-Away Bar again."

"What did he tell you in the bar?"

"I told him I was done and that I wasn't really a hitman but an over-the road-truck driver just looking to buy my own rig."

"What did he say when you told him that?"

"Jimmy said he didn't care what I did. He just wanted his wife dead. Later that evening we went for a ride

188

in his car. He suddenly pulled into his driveway. He removed a gas can from his trunk and set the house on fire."

"So you witnessed him committing Arson?"

"Yes, I did. When I saw Jimmy pouring the gas around the foundation of his residence I took off running. I read later in the paper he crashed his car and was arrested."

"How much alcohol do you think Jimmy had consumed before he started the arson fire?"

"A lot. He had been drinking whiskey in the bar and in his car. We almost hit a couple taking a walk with their dog over on 5th Street."

"Did Jimmy say anything when he removed the gas can from his car?"

"Yes. He pulled out the gas can and angrily said, 'I'll show that gold digger a thing or two!' Like I said, I got the hell out of there at that point."

"Tell me about Jimmy going to Mrs. Sinclair's safe house."

"Jimmy wanted his gun back and told me to meet him at his residence. I told him no that his wife was there. He said she had moved out."

"Did you believe him?"

"Yes, I did. I met him at his house and gave him back the gun. Jimmy told me her new address and said that he was on his way to kill her himself."

"Go on," prompted Mike.

"I ran out of his house first. The car I stole from the airport had a built-in GPS voice activated system. It led me to her new location. I ran in screaming 'Jimmy has a gun, he has a gun and is going to kill you!'

"Where was Jimmy?"

"He was right behind me holding his gun in his hand."

"I ran to the only light visible in the house which was upstairs. That's when she pointed her gun and made us get on the floor. Please, Detective, go ask her if I tried to warn her."

Mike turned off the tape recorder and left the room with his cell phone.

"Hello, Kathy. I have a question. When those 2 men barged into your house did someone yell he had a gun?"

"I did hear someone yelling really loud about something."

"What did you hear?"

"My TV was on so the voice was muffled."

"Thanks. I'll call you again soon."

Mike put his cell phone back in his pocket, re-entered the room, turned the recorder back on and asked, "How did Jimmy Sinclair know where his wife moved to?"

"I don't know but he told me the address."

"We may need you to wear a wire."

"Why? I recorded our first conversation at The Hide-Away Bar about him hiring me to kill her. The recorder and tape are in my top dresser drawer."

Mike just about fell out of his chair. He couldn't believe what he just heard. "*You what*? Say that again!"

"Before Jimmy gave me the $15,000 in the bank parking lot we agreed to meet at the Hide-Away Bar. I stopped at Radio Shack and bought a tape recorder and put it in my shirt pocket along with several ink pens."

"Why would you tape record the conversation?"

"To protect me. I knew I was never going to go along with killing her and thought I would mail the tape to the police when I left town," said John.

"What is on the tape?"

"At the bar I asked Jimmy, 'Do you want it in the head or torso'? And he said torso."

Mike called his partner and told him to pick up the tape recorder inside the dresser and bring it back to him.

"Have you ever been in trouble with law enforcement anywhere?"

"Nope. I'm clean."

Mike turned to the lawyer. "Wait here until that tape arrives. If what your client just told me under oath is on the tape you can leave with him." Mike then left the room.

Harry entered John's apartment along with the ID technician and the old man who manages the units.

The detective opened the top drawer and among the white socks and underwear in plain view were a small tape recorder and tape.

The tech took a few photos and Harry put the recorder and tape in a transparent evidence bag.

He recovered the stash of loot from under the dresser and also took a bag of chocolates that John had left open on his coffee table.

Mike called Kathy from the police station hallway. "Hello, Kathy this is Mike - good news maybe."

"What good news, Baby?"

"I said *maybe* not B*aby*."

"I know you said *maybe. I* said B*aby."*

"Are you flirting with me?"

"Yes, Mike, I am. Soon I'll be free and rich but I don't want to be alone."

"With your pretty face and body you won't have to worry about being alone."

"What good news do you have for me, Baby?" Kathy asked in a sexy voice.

"We made a deal with the hitman to turn state's evidence against Jimmy. He told us how your husband hired him."

"When and why?"

"At the Hide-Away Bar a few weeks ago. Jimmy said you were a gold digger and didn't love him."

"He is right on both counts."

"The hitman claims he tape-recorded their first meeting."

"Do you have the tape?"

"My partner is on the way to the station now with the recorder."

"Is there anything I can do?"

"Yes. I need you to come down and listen to the voice on the tape to confirm the voice as Jimmy's."

"Ok."

"I also need you to identify his handwriting because he gave the hitman your work schedule."

"I can be there shortly."

"I'll have Harry meet you in the lobby."

"Okay, Baby, I'll be there in 20 minutes."

Mike laughed and walked back into the interview room. He turned the recorder back on. "How did you steal cars from the long-term parking lot?"

"I read in the paper where thieves were stealing cars from movie theater parking lots - giving them a 2 hour head start before they were reported missing."

"But why the airport?"

"I saw an airplane in the air and thought about the long-term parking lot. I started talking to people exiting their cars and found out how long they would be gone."

Mike's partner popped his head in and motioned for him to come out. He turned the recorder off and left the room.

"Here's all the cash we found plus the recorder," said Harry almost out of breath. "There is at least $60,000 and I played the tape."

Mike removed the recorder from the police evidence bag and rewound the small tape. He then hit the play button. Two voices were on it and he knew right away to whom both voices belonged.

Mike heard: "Sorry I'm late. I had another argument with Kathy. I know the police will be checking my bank accounts for any transactions once Kathy is killed. I can't have any out of the ordinary withdraws. So I thought of a good way to give you your required down payment."

"What good way is that?"

"After I visit with Kathy's divorce lawyer I want you to meet me at Summit Bank. I'll give you half of the $30,000 we agreed on and the other half once she is dead. Now did you visit my store and check my wife out?"

"Yep. A very attractive woman, maybe 15 years younger than you."

"Kathy's 26 and I am 45. Can you make it look like a store robbery?

"That's my work. You want her shot in the head or torso?"

"The torso will do. I have to go to our meeting. It starts at 10. I have to pretend I want to settle."

Mike turned to his partner. "Get Jimmy and his lawyer into an interview room please."

"Will do."

"Place the cash into property and then call me when Kathy Sinclair arrives."

Mike returned to John's interview room and played the tape. When finished he turned to attorney McKinsey. "You can take your client with you. Get me all his contact numbers in case we need to get in touch with him again."

The detective turned to John. "This tape is allowing you to walk free but stay out of trouble," he warned.

Mike was paged to return to the Detective Bureau. His partner had a visitor. He walked in and saw a large crowd of detectives standing around his desk.

Sitting there was Kathy in a sexy outfit. Harry was standing next to her with a clipboard. Mike tried to act all official but the men saw through his act.

"Get back to work," Mike glared at his men while holding out his hand to Kathy. His tone then softened. "Thank you, Mrs. Sinclair, for coming down on such short notice."

Both shook hands. "Let's go into interview room 4." Kathy stood up and all eyes were on her as she walked into room 4.

Mike had her sit down. He whispered to her that the guys were watching from the observation room. He then turned the microphone on.

"Thanks again for coming down, Mrs. Sinclair. I have an audio tape we found. Can you identify any of the voices?"

Mike played the tape and right away Kathy said, "That's Jimmy talking. Can I listen to the tape?"

"Of course. I have to warn you that your spouse is talking about having you killed."

Mike laid a piece of paper in front of her showing the store schedule work hours. "Is this Jimmy's handwriting?"

"Yes. He writes worse than a doctor filling out a prescription."

"Jimmy and his lawyer will soon be in interview room number 1. Care to watch from the observation room?"

"Wow! May I?"

"I'll be back in a few minutes to get you. Just stay here and listen to the tape. Don't touch the recorder. It's my only copy."

"I won't touch it."

"Good. See you in a few minutes."

He then entered the observation room.

It was crowded with detectives. "Get back to work you horny wolves," Mike said motioning with his hands.

"What a Fox!" one detective said.

"My last victim was 75, hunchbacked and overweight," said another.

A police officer said, "That sounds like the Chief's wife!"

"Guess you don't mind working overtime on this one," said Detective Tony Malone to Mike.

"Someone has to protect and serve, Tony. Might as well be me."

Mike brought Kathy into the viewing room. He gave her a yellow pad and pen. "Take some notes and I will be back in to get them." Mike picked up the tape recorder and left the room.

BUSTED

Mike and Harry entered interview room 1 and introduced themselves to Attorney Ron Lothamen, a well-known criminal defense attorney who loved being on television.

They all sat down and Ron turned to his client and said, "Don't say a word."

"Jimmy, I am charging you with a second count of attempted murder. Your hitman just gave us a full confession. We know your 38 revolver slugs match the slugs recovered at your store and on the exterior wall of your home. We recovered the $50,000 in cash you paid your hitman to kill your wife. We have..."

Attorney Lothamen motioned with his hands for the detective to stop. "First of all my client is innocent of all charges. You know he filed a stolen gun report and the money you recovered was a loan to John Farran so that he could buy an 18 wheeler and go into business for himself."

"We know the money was not for a loan. It was for a contract killing," said Harry.

"On the first arrest for attempted murder my client was kidnapped by this John Farran."

"Kidnapped? Don't make me laugh, said Harry as he opened a bag of chips.

"My client was forced to drink alcohol until drunk. He was forced into his car and driven to the scene of his own house fire."

"A fire he set himself but go on with his story," said Mike.

"It is not a story, Detective. The so called hitman crashed the car and put him behind the wheel. My client says he ran into the house to warn Kathy that this man was trying to kill her."

"No, Mr. Lothamen, under oath, John Farran told us he was with your client when he pulled up to Jimmy's house. That your client pulled out a gas can and said, 'I'll show that gold digger a thing or two'. The victim says that it was John that warned her that Jimmy had the gun," said Harry.

Mike pulled out the small tape recorder. "You can tell your story to the jury. We have your client's fingerprints on the gas can. We have the gas station attendant's statement that your client purchased the gas and gas container. Now we have this bit of evidence."

Mike rewound the tape. "The hitman recorded his conversation about the hit with your client in the Hide-Away Bar."

Mike pushed play and Jimmy's voice could be heard.

"Sorry I'm late. I had another fight with Kathy. I know the police will be checking my bank account for any transactions once Kathy is killed. I can't have any out of the ordinary withdraws. So I thought of a good way to give you your required down payment."

"What good way is that?"

"After I visit with Kathy's divorce lawyer I want you to meet me at Summit Bank. I'll give you half of the $30,000 we agreed on and the other half once she is dead. Now did you visit my store and check my wife out?"

"Yep. A very attractive woman. Maybe 15 years younger than you."

"Kathy's 26 and I am 45. Can you make it look like a store robbery?"

"That's my work. You want her shot in the head or torso?"

"The torso will do. I have to go to our meeting. It starts at 10. I have to pretend I want to settle."

Mike turned the recorder off as Harry smiled at Jimmy and his high-priced lawyer.

"Can you give me a minute alone with my client please?"

"You mean your *innocent* client?" said Harry while slapping a 'Buy 6 Get 6 Free' donut ad on the table in front of Jimmy before walking out behind his partner.

The lawyer picked up the ad and asked "What's this all about?"

"The donut ad is a joke. He never stops eating."

"Sounds like the detectives have a strong case with the recording of you soliciting the man to kill your wife. Now tell me the whole truth."

"I did hire a hitman to kill my wife but after the drive-by shooting failed I told him to stop."

"Did he stop?"

No. He's crazy. He demanded $35,000 more on top of the $15,000 I gave him."

Jimmy became increasingly agitated. "I paid him off but like I said he's crazy. He kidnapped me, got me drunk and set my house on fire. When I made bail I went to my house to tell my wife the truth. I didn't know she had already moved out. The hitman stood in the doorway and said he was on his way to kill her. I followed him to warn her. Kathy held us at gunpoint. That's the truth."

The attorney was a veteran but this was one of the most convoluted situations he had heard about in some time. "Let me see about getting you released on bail in the morning."

"In the morning? Why not right now?" Jimmy whined.

"Sorry, but it doesn't work like that. We have procedures to follow."

Ronald pushed a call button and both detectives entered the room. "Okay, Gentlemen, I'll see you at the bond hearing in the morning."

"The State Attorney will be asking for no bail due to the 2nd attempt on the victim's life," said Harry with a smile.

The attorney turned to his client. "Jimmy, get a good night's sleep. I'll see you at the bond hearing."

Harry quickly opened the interview room door and motioned for a uniformed officer. "Take this man back to his cell." He closed the door after Jimmy was escorted out.

"Gentlemen, I will be fighting hard for my client to make bond. He has never been in trouble with the law before and has been an active member of the community all his life."

"That may be true, Sir, but this is the 2nd time in a few days where Jimmy has attempted to kill his wife."

"He says he tried to stop the hit."

"He has the financial resources to still carry it out. Under these circumstances we will argue that he remain behind bars," replied Mike.

"We have even more evidence than the first arrest," added Harry as he strained over his girth to tie his shoelaces.

Jimmy made one phone call before entering his cell. Donna showed up at visiting hours and they talked over phones separated by thick glass.

"It doesn't look good for me. The hitman I stupidly hired, then fired, tape recorded our first conversation and the police have the tape of me wanting her killed."

"You tried to stop the violence, Honey and the police know that. When the judge hears the whole story they will give you probation."

"I do hope so. I promise that once this is all behind me you will be Mrs. Jimmy Sinclair."

Kathy returned to her mansion and called John on her cell. "According to the detectives the State Attorney will argue for no bond. Your plan, John or what I call 'our scheme' is falling into place."

"Soon you will be a rich and free woman and I'll be in a new 18 wheeler driving on the road again."

Mike and Harry rushed to the courthouse just as the prosecutor was playing the audio tape where Jimmy vented his desire to have his wife killed.

Judge Cummings listened and made his ruling. The detectives left the courtroom smiling.

Mike called Kathy. "You can relax. We played the judge the recording that John Farran made and the judge pounded his gavel over and over and said 'No bond'."

"Thank God. What's going to happen next?" Kathy asked.

"The State Attorney will prosecute Jimmy and he will go to jail."

"I was thinking of dropping the charges if Jimmy settled our divorce fairly. He pleads guilty, gets probation and stays out of my life."

"Well you are the victim. You could have your divorce attorney make an offer to his criminal lawyer."

"I think I'll do that tomorrow. It doesn't hurt to discuss all my options."

She called Mike back about 10 minutes later. "By the way, I am throwing a 'he's busted party'."

"Really!"

"Yes. I will be inviting you and Harry. I will call you with the party time."

"We will be there," Mike said.

Kathy began to call people and invite them to her party. At the top of her list was Mike Anderson.

ON THE ROAD AGAIN

John rode the Metro bus to Comcar Truck Sales and started walking the huge lot. He climbed in and out of many new and used 18 wheeler rigs.

A salesman approached and stuck out his hand. "Pete Mitchell. Welcome to Comcar Truck Sales."

John shook the man's hand as the eager salesman asked, "Can we make a sale today?"

John replied, "I may come into some money soon and if I do I'll be back to pick something up."

"Good to hear that. Here's my card. Just look all you want. If you have any questions, any at all, just call me."

"I would like to fill out a credit application while I am here."

"Ok. Find the truck you want to purchase, then see me in my office."

John went back to climbing in and out of his future ride. While sitting in a brand new Volvo 380 eighteen-wheeler he called his best trucking friend.

"Hey, Byron, it's John."

"Dude, where have you been? My rig you want to buy is sitting out in front of my double wide trailer."

"That's why I'm calling. I came into some money and I plan to buy a new Volvo 380 instead of your Gulfstream."

"Wow, Dude, a Volvo 380 – that's over $100,000!"

"I know, I know!" John exclaimed.

"If you buy it bring it by. I'll be shotgun on your first run!" said Byron excitedly.

"Shotgun – I thought partner-in my own truck line called 'John Farran Trucking', with our motto 'Get It There on Time'."

"Wow, Dude, you mean it?"

"Come on Byron we've been best friends since high school. We've done everything together so why not this?"

"Get off the phone, Dude, and get your butt out here to Little Rock."

"Okay, Partner. I'll try to be in Little Rock soon." John hung up his cell phone and took the wheel on his new ride.

Kathy removed her TV dinner from the microwave and walked to the living room. On the evening news a reporter was interviewing Steve Conners.

Kathy called her mother and a few of her friends. She told them to watch the newscast. "My husband was arrested for attempted murder."

"Here with me in an exclusive interview is private investigator Steve Conners. He shot the video you are about to see. His client hired him because she was afraid of her husband, who, at this very moment sits in the county jail charged with attempted murder."

Kathy watched the clip of the police arriving with blue lights and sirens and the arrest of both her husband and John. The video ended with both men handcuffed in the backseat of police cars.

The phone rang. It was John on the other end.

"Hi, John."

"Hi, Kathy. Are you watching the news?"

"Yes."

"I'd like to celebrate but I can't be seen with you being an alleged hitman and all. Besides, the deal I made with the State Attorney requires me to leave the city and only come back for the trial."

"Well, my Mother will wire tomorrow the $15,000 the police confiscated tonight to your brother's bank in New Mexico."

"Thanks. Good luck with your divorce," said John. "I'll send you a few photos once I am on the road."

"Ok. By the way, I'm going on a 14 day cruise to the Virgin Islands. I leave Sunday."

"Being on a ship sounds like fun but I'd rather be in my eighteen-wheeler listing to country music and seeing the good old USA."

"John. I always wondered why you came to Tupelo. You have no family here."

"When I was trucking I passed through Tupelo on my weekly run from Montgomery to Memphis. I love Elvis music and he was born there so I said to myself, 'Let's go to Tupelo'."

"Thanks for saving my life. Enjoy your travels on the road and send me that photo."

"One more thing, Kathy. What about my $5,000 bonus for staying?"

"I haven't forgotten our agreement. I will place the money in a locker at the airport tomorrow. I'll put the key in an envelope and leave it under your door mat."

"Thanks, Kathy. Enjoy the Love Boat."

A lot of people showed up at Kathy's lavish party.

The caterer's granddaughters were distributing t-shirts to all the guests. There were at least 40 people in her house.

Steve walked over to his new client who was standing next to Mike and handed Kathy her cruise ticket. "Thanks to your case I made the news and the exposure brought me more work."

"Good! Do you know Detective Anderson?"

"Yes. Hi, Sir. I dropped off my videos and reports to your office just prior to coming here."

"Thanks, Steve. If you have business cards please give me some. I know a lot of people."

Steve handed over a stack and strolled over to the buffet table where Harry was piling food onto his plate.

"Try the roast beef," said Harry as he took another bite himself.

Billy Sutton walked over to his boss who was laughing at something Mike was saying.

"Yes, Billy?" Kathy asked.

"Ma'am, I need the keys to the store so I can open tomorrow for you."

"Of course. They're hanging on a hook in the laundry room. A small bear is attached to the keys."

As Billy walked away she turned her attention to Mike. "I made Billy my manager. He'll do a good job while I'm on my cruise."

"When is that cruise and where is it going?" he asked.

"It leaves the day after tomorrow. I fly to Atlanta then connect in Miami. I have a free shuttle to the cruise port. I sail on the Carnival ship 'Sensation' for a wonderful two weeks in the Virgin Islands."

"Wow! Sounds like a lot of fun!"

"Why don't you come, Mike? It's a cruise for single people. Steve Connors is who I bought my ticket from."

"I can't. Too many crimes to solve. I wish I could go. It sounds like it would be a blast."

Several customers from the grocery store approached wearing their special shirts given to everyone.

"We love the t-shirts. We feel it's a souvenir," 2 ladies said, laughing.

Mike laughed as the women walked away. "It is a funny t-shirt." Mike held his own t-shirt up. On the front was a man behind bars. Below the image was the word 'busted'.

"I hope your partner can fit into the largest size I could find which was a triple x," laughed Kathy.

Mike spotted his partner holding a plate full of food. He was talking to several middle-aged ladies.

"I've been on his case to get back in shape but he's not listening," said Mike.

Kathy's cell phone rang. Steve was on the other end. "Kathy, I almost forgot. I'm treating you to a free limo ride to the airport. It will pick you up at 9 A.M. Again, thanks for everything and have a fun time."

Kathy replied, "Wow! Thanks!" and hung up.

"Who was that?" asked Mike.

"It was Steve. He's treating me to my 1st limo ride on Sunday."

"He'll go far. He knows how to service his customers," said Mike while watching his partner stuff his face with more catered food.

Harry was having a hard time deciding which of the 3 ladies to ask out. They all knew Harry was a detective and this fact excited the women.

Harry had ferreted out some details of his 3 choices. Sandra was a petite waitress in a small diner in the next town over. Rebecca was tall, had graduated from an east coast institution and was a bookkeeper for a local accounting firm. Christy was a well-endowed nurse.

'So many choices, who will be the lucky woman to land me'?" Harry mused.

He picked up his dessert plate with a large piece of cheesecake just begging to be eaten.

He started to take a bite when conscientious nurse Christy took the fork from Harry's hand and softly said, "You don't need that, Honey."

She removed the plate from the hands of a very surprised Harry. Christy took him by the arm and escorted him away from the dessert table.

"Let's go for a walk instead," she said as she guided him out to the pool area filling his ears with statistics from the newly revised food pyramid.

On Sunday, a black Lincoln limo pulled up to Kathy's residence right on time. The sharply dressed driver rang the bell and later carried 2 suitcases to the trunk.

Carol gave her daughter a hug as the driver opened the passenger door and Kathy climbed in.

"Good morning," said a man's voice from inside the limo.

Kathy adjusted her eyes to the dark interior and noticed a man sitting there dressed in jeans and a polo shirt.

"Mike! This is a surprise. What are you doing in my limo?"

"I'm going on the cruise too!"

"How did you get the time off?"

"My commander has been bugging me to slow down for months, so I went in his office yesterday and said I was taking 2 weeks off. I called Steve and he was happy I purchased a ticket from him."

They talked and laughed as their limo traveled slowly through the downtown section of Tupelo. The driver stopped in front of Buffalo Bill's Grocery Store as instructed.

"I'll only be a minute."

"Okay. Bring me a pack of gum please - any brand will do."

"Alright," Kathy said as she closed the limo door.

Inside, everything was in place and very clean. She walked up to Billy and laughed. He was wearing the 'Busted' t-shirt.

"Nice shirt, Billy!"

"Hi, Mrs. Sinclair. I've sold more t-shirts than meat this morning."

"Great. You have my Mom's phone number right?" Kathy asked.

"Yes, Boss, I do." Billy said. "I may be pushing my luck but can I also drive your BMW while you're away?"

"Why not? The keys are in a cookie jar in my kitchen. Water my house plants when you stop by," Kathy said.

'Will do, Boss."

Kathy picked up several packs of gum and left.

Billy smiled and shouted, "Have a fun time!"

Inside the limo Kathy handed Mike his gum and they kissed. "I've wanted to do that for a long time," Mike said as he opened a pack of gum.

Kathy laughed and replied, "Me too."

As their limo drove through town towards the airport Kathy spotted Harry. He was walking with a woman from the party. Their limo stopped just as Harry and the woman entered a business.

Kathy and Mike started laughing at the same time when they noticed the sign above the business, 'Weight Watchers'.

"Good for him, good for him," Mike repeated as he slid closer to Kathy. They were in the midst of enjoying the next lingering kiss when Kathy's cell phone rang.

It was her expensive attorney. "Hi, Kathy, Paul Salman here."

"Hello, Sir."

"I just got off the phone with Jimmy's defense attorney Ron Lothamer."

"Really! That was fast. What did you discuss?"

"The State Attorney will accept our offer of us dropping charges and allowing Jimmy to receive probation instead of jail. Jimmy has to give you a quick divorce and $4 million in cash."

"Fantastic news, Sir"

"We will have to run this deal by the Judge but between us he owes me a bunch of favors."

"When will you know for sure?"

"I should be able to give you the court's decision when you return from your cruise."

"I am so happy, Paul. I knew you were the best divorce attorney around!"

"It's not a done deal yet but have a fun time and relax."

Kathy gave Mike an extra big kiss and told him the news.

"Wow! $4 million! Way to go, Girl."

Their kissing intensified as the limo headed south toward the airport.

Janet was sunbathing by her apartment complex pool when she heard a man's voice say, "Hello."

She raised her head and observed a very good-looking UPS driver holding a small box.

"Are you, Janet Lee?"

"Yes."

"I have a package I need you to sign for," the shy driver stated.

Janet immediately took an interest in the muscular young man and made an effort to observe his name tag as she made her way over to him.

"Who is the package from? Norman."

The shy employee glanced from the approaching woman to the package and responded. "From Belinda Lee in Hong Kong."

Janet took the package, signed in the designated area and took the liberty of informing the driver, "Belinda is one of my 7 sisters!"

She could tell the young man was shy and knew she would have to be the aggressor if she was going to get anywhere.

'Mike had his chance. He doesn't know what he's missing! Oh well, no time like the present and nothing to lose'.

"Say, Norman, are you by any chance single?"

"Yes I am."

A shiny new eighteen-wheeler with 'John Farran Trucking' and 'Get It There on Time' was headed north on Highway 78 from Tupelo to Memphis.

Behind the wheel was John Farran. He was enjoying every minute of his trip. The county jail was on his left with about 30 men in the exercise yard when he loudly blasted his air horn 3 or 4 times.

Jimmy, wearing a bright orange county jail uniform looked up from playing checkers and saw John's new rig heading north.

"Son of a bitch," said Jimmy just as Leroy made multiple jumps and took half of his checkers.

Laughing as he shifted gears John picked up his CB radio and said, "This is John the Hitman-come back."

The End

OPTIONAL BOOK ENDING

Harry was sitting at his desk eating his third apple when Steve and Aaron walked in at 8 AM on Monday morning.

Steve was holding two CD's in his left hand. He joked, "Can I have a bite, Detective?"

Harry did not answer.

Steve placed the 2 CD's down in front of Harry and asked, "Where can we watch this short 3 minute video my rookie, Aaron, shot between Friday and Saturday?"

Harry with his mouth still full grabbed another apple off his desk and motioned for both men to follow him.

They climbed 3 flights of stairs to the coffee room instead of taking the quicker elevator.

Harry finished his apple and said, "Trying to get in shape for the new woman in my life."

"It's working," replied Steve-patting his own small gut.

"What are we going to watch?" quizzed Harry who was now by the CD player attached to a large flat screen television.

Steve just smiled and said "Surprise, surprise, surprise."

Harry pushed a few buttons and the large screen came to life. He saw a green BMW in the flow of traffic near a sign showing 'Tupelo Airport-One Mile'. The date on the video was only a few days ago.

"What is on this video, Steve?"

The PI instructed his rookie to tell Harry the entire story.

Aaron reached for the TV remote in Harry's hand. "May I have the remote, Sir?"

Harry handed the controller over.

"I really want to be a private investigator. Steve instructed me to go to Wal-Mart and discretely film people leaving the store. Then I was to follow them all the way home."

"And?" asked Harry.

"So I was doing that all Friday morning when I happened to observe Kathy in traffic. For fun I decided to follow her."

"And?" said Harry moving his hands.

"Kathy did not go home. She went to the Tupelo Airport instead."

Harry impatiently interrupted Aaron from telling the whole story. "Young man, I do not have all day."

Aaron started the video again and all 3 watched Kathy walk into the airport. She went directly to a storage locker holding a thick white envelope in her right hand.

The video showed her place the envelope into locker number 28. She locked it and removed the key. She then put the key into a smaller envelope, sealed it and exited the terminal.

Aaron stopped the video and said, "I lost her in traffic so I went back and staked out the locker. On Saturday morning someone finally showed up."

Steve turned to Harry and smiled. "Guess who showed up?"

Harry shrugged his shoulders a few times and said, "I have no idea. Who showed up?"

Steve laughed and replied, "Surprise, surprise, surprise."

Aaron pushed the play button again. John Farran is now on the video reaching into locker number 28 and removing the large white envelope.

"I don't believe what I am witnessing," said Harry.

The camera zoomed in on a large wad of cash being counted by the truck driver. John then placed the cash into a gym bag and exited the terminal.

Aaron turned the TV off.

"I lost him in traffic so I went right over to Economy Travel and waited for my boss to return."

Steve looked at Harry and said, "I made 3 copies. Two are for you and one I need for my official file on Jimmy Sinclair. This video shows that Kathy and John know each other."

"It sure does," said a smiling Harry.

"My rookie did a great job staking out the locker all on his own. Right?"

Harry said, "Aaron, you did a great job. I like your dedication to your boss. Kathy sure had me fooled. She has some explaining to do when she returns from her cruise."

Harry instructed them to keep quiet about their video. He escorted them down 6 flights of stairs to the lobby.

They shook hands and said their goodbyes. Harry then climbed the 3 flights of stairs to the detective bureau.

Outside the police station, Aaron said to Steve, "I want to go to Wal-Mart and follow people."

"Go ahead, and Aaron, you just earned a $5.00 an hour raise."

Aaron did a huge fist pump and ran to his white van.

Harry called Steve on his cell phone. "I am watching your man run to his van from my 3rd floor window. You have a good employee there."

Steve looked up and waved. "Thanks Harry. What is your next step?"

"First. I want you to find me a cruise to go on next month with my girlfriend."

"I can do that."

"Work wise, I will take a ride over to the jail and interview Jimmy Sinclair."

Steve gave the detective a thumbs up and departed the area.

Harry called Jimmy's lawyer and told him about the CD but not was on it. They agreed to meet at the jail.

On the way Harry stopped at his favorite Subway Sandwich Shop. He ordered a foot long Ham and Cheese on wheat bread and purchased a bottle of water.

The clerk asked, "No chips, cookies or soda, Detective?"

"No junk in the trunk," replied Harry as he paid for his meal.

Jimmy and his lawyer were waiting in interview room number 2 when Harry walked in with a small CD player. He popped in a CD and pushed pause.

"What is on the CD, Detective?" asked Attorney Lothamen.

Harry smiled and replied, "Surprise, surprise, surprise. The video you 2 are going to view is about 3 minutes long. Just watch and when it's over I will explain."

Harry pushed play and all 3 watched Kathy place a large envelope into locker number 28 and John retrieving the envelope and counting the money.

Harry turned off the CD player and removed the CD and handed it to Ron. "This is your copy. Are you surprised about the video?"

"I am shocked. This video clearly proves Kathy Sinclair and John Farran know each other. This must be some kind of payoff."

Jimmy cannot hold back his emotions any longer and blurts out, "I told you I did not set my house on fire, that John got me drunk and crashed my car."

Harry explained how he obtained the video. "A rookie PI who works for

Steve Conners spotted Kathy in traffic and followed her. On his own he staked out the locker till John arrived."

"What now? Detective."

"I will bring her and John Farran in and get to the bottom of this."

Harry stood up and adjusted his belt. "Ron, you can ask for bail for your client. I will not object this time. Just keep very quiet about this video."

Ron placed his copy of the CD into his briefcase and turned to Harry. "I see that you lost some weight."

"Yes. 8 pounds and counting."

Harry looks over at Jimmy and says, "No more donuts for me."

Jimmy stands up and shakes Harry's hand.

Ron speaks next. "Thanks for showing us this CD."

"You both are welcome. My new girlfriend is turning me into a slim and trim nice guy." Harry then smiled and exited the interview room.

Ron explained to Jimmy that he will be released on bail in the morning. A jailer escorted him back to his cell.

Jimmy said to the jailer, "I am being released tomorrow." The jailer said nothing and placed the prisoner back into his cell. Leroy had a game of checkers ready on the lower bunk.

Jimmy spoke as he made the first move, "I bail out tomorrow. My lawyer has new evidence."

Kathy and Mike were sipping white wine with their dinners. She was dressed in a pretty pink dress and he was in a black tuxedo he rented.

The Captain stood up and spoke to the large dinner crowd. "Ladies and Gentlemen this is your Captain speaking. Tomorrow morning when you wake up we will be docked in St. Thomas."

Mike and Kathy tapped their glasses together. He turned to her and said, "Twelve more days of fun and sun and then it's back to the rat race."

John is underneath his new semi changing out the oil when Byron Allen walks in with a portable telephone. "Hey, John, it's your lawyer."

John wipes his hands and says, Hello, Joe."

"Hello, John. How is Little Rock?"
"Windy, but it feels good to be standing here with my buddy. We leave tomorrow for Dallas on a truck run."

"Well, John, you will have to cancel that trip and come back to Tupelo. Detective Harry Fusco needs to interview you. He wants to see us within 48 hours. It seems they have new evidence."

"Did the detective say what new evidence?"

"No. All he said was surprise, surprise, surprise."

John just stood there in the garage with a puzzled look on his face.

* * THE END * *

CPSIA information can be obtained
at www.ICGtesting.com
Printed in the USA
FSHW01n2149270418
47403FS